Her Baby
and Her Beau

Victoria Pade

WITHDRAWN

If you purchased this book without a cover you should be aware
that this book is stolen property. It was reported as "unsold and
destroyed" to the publisher, and neither the author nor the
publisher has received any payment for this "stripped book."

Recycling programs
for this product may
not exist in your area.

ISBN-13: 978-0-373-65866-4

Her Baby and Her Beau

Copyright © 2015 by Victoria Pade

All rights reserved. Except for use in any review, the reproduction or
utilization of this work in whole or in part in any form by any electronic,
mechanical or other means, now known or hereinafter invented, including
xerography, photocopying and recording, or in any information storage
or retrieval system, is forbidden without the written permission of the
publisher, Harlequin Enterprises Limited, 225 Duncan Mill Road,
Don Mills, Ontario M3B 3K9, Canada.

This is a work of fiction. Names, characters, places and incidents are
either the product of the author's imagination or are used fictitiously,
and any resemblance to actual persons, living or dead, business
establishments, events or locales is entirely coincidental.

This edition published by arrangement with Harlequin Books S.A.

For questions and comments about the quality of this book,
please contact us at CustomerService@Harlequin.com.

® and TM are trademarks of Harlequin Enterprises Limited or its
corporate affiliates. Trademarks indicated with ® are registered in the
United States Patent and Trademark Office, the Canadian Intellectual
Property Office and in other countries.

Printed in U.S.A.

www.Harlequin.com

Victoria Pade is a *USA TODAY* bestselling author. A native of Colorado, she's lived there her entire life. She studied art before discovering her real passion was for writing, and even after more than eighty books, she still loves it. When she isn't writing she's baking and worrying about how to work off the calories. She has better luck with the baking than with the calories. Readers can contact her on her Facebook page.

Books by Victoria Pade

Harlequin Special Edition

The Camdens of Colorado

To Catch a Camden
A Camden Family Wedding
It's a Boy!
A Baby in the Bargain
Corner-Office Courtship

Montana Mavericks: Rust Creek Cowboys

The Maverick's Christmas Baby

Northbridge Nuptials

A Baby for the Bachelor
The Bachelor's Northbridge Bride
Marrying the Northbridge Nanny
The Bachelor, the Baby and the Beauty
The Bachelor's Christmas Bride
Big Sky Bride, Be Mine!
Mommy in the Making
The Camden Cowboy

Montana Mavericks: Striking It Rich

A Family for the Holidays

Visit the Author Profile page at Harlequin.com for more titles.

Prologue

Standing at the front door to his grandmother's Denver home on that sizzling August afternoon, Beau Camden heard a car pull up the drive behind him.

He spun around so fast he might as well have still been in the caves of Afghanistan with a rifle in his hands.

Then he recognized his older brother Cade at the wheel of a blue sedan and relaxed.

Beau watched as Cade parked behind his own black SUV, thinking that maybe Cade would have better luck getting someone to answer the door.

"Beau! Hey!" Cade called as he got out of his car and headed for the landing. "I didn't expect to see you."

"GiGi asked me to come over. But I rang the bell and knocked, and no one seems to be here."

Cade raised his chin knowingly. "Oh, that's right, GiGi said you'd been doing that—knocking and ringing the bell instead of just coming in. Acting like you don't belong here—that's what she calls it. She doesn't like it. This is home, pal. *Our* home—we grew up here, remember? I know you've been gone a long time, but nothing's changed. We don't stand on ceremony."

But standing on ceremony had been ingrained in him in the Marines.

And he *had* been gone a long time. Thirteen years. The first four of them in college at Annapolis with summers and holidays spent on the Camden ranch in Northbridge, Montana, to toughen up. The last nine years a marine.

Once a marine, always a marine...

"Hard to get back to things," he muttered.

An understatement.

Beau was having a lot of trouble fitting in again. The few occasions over the years when he'd been home on leave had been vacations from reality. Every waking hour had been filled with activities and seeing family and friends who all wanted to spoil him and show him a good time before he left again.

Being back for good was something else.

When Cade joined him at the oversize front door with its arched top and the stained glass in the upper half he reached in front of Beau, punched in the code that unlocked the door and unceremoniously turned the handle.

"Finally! It's about time, Beaumont Anthony Camden!" came a victorious call from inside before the door was open all the way. "I thought I was going to have to stand here till dark before you got the idea!"

Georgianna Camden, matriarch of the Camden family and the woman who had raised all ten of her grandchildren—the grandmother they called GiGi—stood several feet inside the entry, facing the door as if she'd been there all along.

Spotting Cade, she deflated slightly, her shoulders drooping into her dumpling-like shape, her head shaking enough for her salt-and-pepper curls to shimmy and her frustration showing on the lined face that still bore evidence of beauty.

"Oh, Cade..." she said. "I didn't know you were coming—*you* opened the door, didn't you?"

"Well, it's open, so it doesn't really matter, does it?" Cade asked.

Beau knew his older brother was covering for him.

So did GiGi, if her disapproving frown meant anything.

Cade ignored it and said, "I left my sunglasses when we were here Sunday. Just came to pick them up on my way home."

"Ah. We wondered who those belonged to. They're in the kitchen on the counter."

"But you were waiting for Beau?" Cade asked with a glance from GiGi to Beau. "Standing here in the middle of the entry? With a bowl of marshmallows? What's that, his reward if he came in without ringing the bell or knocking?"

"I was waiting for him to come in, yes," GiGi confirmed. "I'm trying to get that stick out of his—"

"GiGi!" Cade teasingly cut her off.

"He keeps acting like a stranger around here. It has to stop!" To Beau she added forcefully, "It *has* to stop!"

"Sorry, ma'am," Beau apologized automatically.

And for that, his grandmother threw a marshmallow at his chest.

Beau's reflexes were lightning quick and he caught it as his grandmother's frustration erupted.

"Every time you call me *ma'am* that's what you're getting!" she warned. "I changed your diapers and wiped your nose and kissed your boo-boos. I am not *ma'am*!"

Cade laughed again and said, "I told you she wants the old Beau back. We all do. The uniform is off. You're just one of us again. That's how we want you to feel."

Beau kept himself from saying the automatic *yes, sir* that was on the tip of his tongue and merely mimicked his brother's earlier tilt of the chin to acknowledge Cade's comment.

But he was thinking, *easier said than done...*

Unsure what else to do with the marshmallow, Beau ate it.

"Is this why you invited him over today?" Cade asked GiGi then. "To keep him hostage here and thump him with marshmallows until he's retrained? *Un*-boot camp? Marshmallow deprogramming?"

"No. I need to talk to him," GiGi said more seriously. "I just decided that from now on I'll leave him cooling his heels on the doorstep until he figures out to come in like everyone else does. And every time he calls me ma'am he *is* going to get *thumped* with one of these," she threatened, jostling the ammunition in her bowl.

Beau thought how like his strong-willed grandmother it was not to accept something she didn't care for. And he made a mental note to try harder not to be so formal with her. With everyone. But his training went deep and he wasn't sure what it was going to take to change that.

His brother's expression sobered suddenly, as if something had occurred to him. "Oh, GiGi, you aren't thinking about sending him out on one of *our* missions, are you? Give him a break—it's too soon for that. He's only been home two months. You can't—"

"There's something he needs to know and he needs to know it *now*," GiGi insisted, sounding determined to conquer an unpleasant task.

"I'm fine," Beau said to Cade, appreciating his brother looking out for him even as it secretly amused him. They weren't kids anymore and he was a long—*long*—way from needing his big brother's protection. Cade was as tall as Beau and in shape, but Beau knew he could have Cade on the ground and out cold before Cade knew what hit him. Certainly there was nothing their seventy-five-year-old grandmother could come up with that he couldn't take in stride.

"I can handle whatever she needs to tell me. Whatever she needs me to do," he assured his brother.

"Don't bet on it," Cade countered.

"I'll be glad for more to do," Beau added, meaning it. He wasn't working for Camden Incorporated yet and had too much idle time on his hands. He was lifting weights and working out for hours these days just to expend his pent-up energy. And even after all that he still couldn't sleep at night.

"We need some privacy to talk," GiGi said to Cade.

"And I'm supposed to make myself scarce, is that it, *ma'am*?" Cade said facetiously.

GiGi threw a marshmallow at him.

Cade's reflexes were good, too, because he also caught the confection, popping it into his mouth before he said, "Come on, GiGi, cut him a little slack—"

"Your sunglasses are in the kitchen," the woman repeated. "Beau and I are going into the den."

For a moment Cade locked eyes with GiGi, but when

she raised one eyebrow at him Beau knew his brother had lost the standoff.

Cade apparently had the same realization. "Looks like there's nothing I can do for you, little brother. You know how she is when she sets her mind to something—"

"More determined than Afghan rebels," Beau confirmed. "But I did all right with those. I think I'll be okay."

"I hope so," Cade said, as if he wasn't too sure. Then to their grandmother he added, "Really, GiGi, give it to someone else—"

"Kitchen," she commanded Cade. Then to Beau she said a definitive, "And you, this way."

"Good luck," Cade said.

"Thanks," Beau responded as they both followed orders, going where they'd been told to go, with GiGi herding Beau into the paneled den.

She closed the door behind them before she let out a deep sigh and moved to the desk.

"Sit," she said, indicating the tufted leather sofa against the wall of the large, stately room.

Beau followed that order, as well.

GiGi unlocked a drawer in the enormous antique mahogany desk in the center of the room and removed what looked like an old leather-bound book. She brought the book and her bowl of marshmallows to sit at the other end of the sofa, angling toward Beau.

"There's something you need to know," she said then. "Something I read in H.J.'s journals just before you were discharged. I wanted to wait to tell you until you really were settled in. But as of today it can't be put off."

Beau knew what his grandmother was talking about when she mentioned H.J.'s journals. Beau's oldest brother, Seth—who ran the Camden ranch in Northbridge and oversaw all the other Camden Incorporated agricultural interests—had come across journals kept by H. J. Camden, Beau's great-grandfather and the founder of the family's fortunes.

H.J.—as well as his son, Hank, and grandsons Mitchum and Howard—had long been accused of ruthless and unscrupulous practices. H.J. had gone to his grave denying all accusations, but apparently his journals told a different story.

Beau had been in Afghanistan when the journals were found, but he'd been told about the information they held. Many things were done that shouldn't have been.

Underhanded deals, backstabbing, string pulling, sabotaging, payoffs, lying and cheating that had cost other people property or livelihoods, that had wrongly altered and sometimes destroyed lives and futures, and even had ripple effects on later generations.

Since finding the journals and realizing the truth, the current Camdens were endeavoring to make amends where amends could be made. It was being done quietly to avoid scandal or lawsuits against Camden Incorporated.

But if Beau was facing the prospect of one of these missions, he was more eager for it than his brother suspected. A mission with a direct target, a plan of action he could devise and put into effect—it was all actually familiar territory to him. And it felt good to have a purpose again.

"Whatever you need, ma'a—" He caught himself when he saw his grandmother reach into the bowl in her lap. "Whatever you need, *GiGi*," he corrected himself with a wry laugh.

But his grandmother's expression remained solemn as she removed her hand from the bowl and went on.

"I'm sorry, Beau. It's been bad enough reading what I've read in H.J.'s journals and learning that some of the worst that's been said of him, of my own husband, of my sons—your dad and your uncle—is true. But this..."

Another sigh. Another shake of her head. Her brow furrowed and she clearly didn't want to reveal whatever it was that she'd discovered.

"It didn't occur to me as I was going along," she said in a quieter voice, "that H.J. had wronged one of his own family..."

Beau watched his grandmother purse her lips and she seemed to age right before his eyes.

But then she bucked up like a good soldier and opened the book she'd taken from the drawer, turning to a page marked with a paper clip.

"I'm going to let you read this for yourself. And all I can do is apologize to you on behalf of H.J. and say that—mistaken or not—he honestly thought he was doing what was best for you..."

She shook her head again. "It's still inexcusable, but that's what was behind it. And I would never—*ever*—have let it happen if I'd have known," she added remorsefully. "When you've finished reading I have to tell you why this is information that couldn't wait even a day longer."

Chapter One

Kyla Gibson moved gingerly to one of the truck-stop motel room's two beds and eased herself onto it to sit with her sore back against the headboard. She couldn't settle into place without flinching at multiple aches, pains, bruises and cuts. Then she pulled a pillow to her lap to prop the sprained wrist that was also throbbing from the strain of using it more than she was supposed to.

It was only eight o'clock on Tuesday night. Even though she was completely worn out it was too early to go to sleep. But she didn't dare turn on the television for fear that it might wake up the two-month-old infant finally asleep in the crib a few feet away.

Immy. Who had been crying since they'd both been released from the hospital and arrived at the motel a little after five.

Having no real experience with babies, Kyla didn't

know why Immy had been so unhappy. She had received a clean bill of health from the hospital, where she'd behaved normally.

But now, at the motel, in Kyla's sole care, Immy hadn't wanted to eat or sleep.

Was it possible for such a tiny baby to understand that something awful had happened? To miss her parents? To realize on some level that she'd lost them?

But if that was the case, wouldn't she have also been inconsolable at the hospital?

It was only since Kyla had taken over tending to the baby that Immy had become so unhappy.

Maybe she knew...

That's what Kyla kept thinking. Maybe Immy sensed that she was now in the hands of someone inept at caring for her, someone who didn't have the foggiest idea what she was doing or how she was going to do what needed to be done from here on.

Or maybe Kyla's own fears and insecurities about this job that was now hers were somehow infecting the baby.

But regardless of the cause, the baby had just gone on crying and crying and crying and Kyla had been useless—too battered, too weak, too afraid she might drop Immy to walk and jiggle her the way her parents had when Immy was upset.

So Kyla had been at a loss. And tired and hurt and frustrated and sad.

And at one point Kyla had just cried right along with Immy.

But she'd finally persuaded Immy to take a few ounces of formula—much less than she was supposed to be eating, but still, something—and then Immy had fallen asleep.

And now here Kyla was, afraid to even breathe.

Terrified, actually, of everything she was facing.

Terrified and terribly, terribly worried that she wasn't going to be able to handle what was now on her plate even once she was well again.

Before this, Kyla had been a childless kindergarten teacher who shared an apartment in the small Montana town of Northbridge with a roommate. She came and went as she pleased. She dated now and then. She and Darla—her roommate and best friend—got along well and had a good time together. She enjoyed the community she'd become a part of. And she lived a simple, uncomplicated life.

A simple, uncomplicated life that she'd left behind a week and a half ago in order to spend the end of her summer vacation in Denver. Rachel—her cousin and only living relative—had invited her, asking her to become the godmother of Rachel's daughter, Immogene.

Kyla had been enjoying her time with the small family that also included Rachel's Australian husband, Eddie Burke. She'd been enjoying watching Rachel with Immy. Enjoying holding Immy herself for a few minutes here and there, awkwardly giving Immy an occasional bottle, then handing her back to one of her parents if Immy fussed.

Kyla had been honored to become Immy's godmother, and had even offered to take Immy to sleep in the guesthouse with her after the christening.

She'd been happy to give Rachel and Eddie a night of romance rekindling and uninterrupted sleep. Immy was down to needing only one feeding during the night, and with the prepared bottle in the fridge and the bottle warmer on the counter, Kyla had been confident she was up to the task. After all, the guesthouse had occupied the top half of the garage just behind the main house and one call over the intercom would have Rachel or Eddie there in minutes if there were any problems.

But instead of Kyla having problems with Immy, the problem had been the fire that started at the very large, luxurious main house.

That horrible night had cost Rachel and Eddie their lives. Kyla barely escaped with Immy from flames that jumped to burn the guesthouse and garage to the ground, too.

Kyla still couldn't believe it had happened...

A tiny whimper from the crib sent a fresh wave of panic through her right then.

Please stay asleep...

Please, please, please...

Kyla sat frozen and closed her eyes as though, if she pretended she was asleep herself, the tiny baby girl might opt not to disturb her.

She knew that was really dumb. But she was desperate.

When there were no more sounds from the crib after a few minutes, Kyla opened her eyes to mere slits to spy on the infant from a distance and found Immy still asleep.

Thank God...

Kyla breathed again. And felt guilty.

It wasn't that she didn't love the adorable baby with her head of wispy copper-colored hair, her enormous blue eyes, her button nose and beautiful Cupid's-bow mouth. Because she did love her. She loved Immy and had envied Rachel. Especially when holding the baby in her arms had stirred old feelings of Kyla's own loss that she'd thought were resolved a decade ago.

But the truth was that she wasn't much more prepared to have a baby now than she had been when she was sixteen.

Only there Immy was, in the crib. All hers now...

Along with the responsibility of managing what Immy had inherited.

A baby. A huge business. What exactly was she supposed to do with either of those things?

Even if she was in tip-top shape, even if she wasn't banged up and grieving the loss of her cousin, it would still be overwhelming. And she honestly didn't know if she could do it. Any of it. All of it.

She closed her eyes again, this time in the futile hope that when she opened them she'd be back home in Northbridge, hearing Rachel's voice on the other end of the phone saying she'd just given birth to Immy...

If she pictured it vividly enough maybe she could turn back time.

The knock on the door startled her and when her eyes shot open again she was, of course, still in the motel room.

Her first thought was that the knock could have disturbed Immy.

Thankfully it hadn't. *Yet.*

Her second thought was that they were in a *truck-stop* motel. Yes, the business had belonged to Immy's parents and Eddie had talked about striving for high standards in everything about his travel centers, but it still didn't seem to Kyla like an ideal place for a woman alone with a baby.

And she certainly wasn't expecting anyone. How could she be, when the only people she knew in Denver now were the few strangers who had offered help since the fire?

She considered ignoring whoever was there and

keeping the door safely closed. But she couldn't risk a second round of those heavy knocks, so she got off the bed as fast as she could and made her way to the window beside the door.

She was careful to only open the drape a crack, just enough for her to peek at whoever was out there before revealing herself.

There were lights in the overhang outside each room's door, so she could see that there was a man just outside.

A really big man. Tall, broad-shouldered, standing ramrod straight, muscles barely contained by a white polo shirt that stretched tightly over his shoulders and biceps.

He didn't look like the truckers she'd seen when she'd arrived. This guy was meticulously groomed and there didn't seem to be a relaxed bone in his impressive body. In fact, between the way he was standing there—almost at attention—and the short cut of his espresso-colored hair, there was something about him that said *military*.

Military and strikingly handsome.

He had a square brow, deep-set eyes that stared straight ahead at the door, a nose that was a little flat across the bridge and somehow ruggedly distinguished, full, sensuous lips and a jawline that a sculptor's knife couldn't have shaped any better.

Good looks—a serial killer's best asset, Kyla thought.

But as he raised his massive fist to knock a second time she decided she was less afraid of a serial killer than of waking Immy, so she poked her entire head past the curtain, opened the window just a crack and said a hushed, "Can I help you?"

His head alone turned in her direction, giving her a fuller view of his face.

Oh yeah, he was fantastic looking...

Now that he was peering directly at her, she could see that those deep-set eyes were an incredible, intense cobalt blue. A remarkable, unusual blue.

And it was those blue eyes that suddenly sparked familiarity.

"Kyla?" he said.

It couldn't be...

"Can I help you?" she repeated as she convinced herself that she was imagining things.

"You don't recognize me?" the man outside said.

"Who are you?" she asked even as she began to think that she knew.

"Beau. Beau Camden," he said.

Despite confirmation, Kyla stared at him in disbelief.

She couldn't help wondering if she was hallucinating. She'd refused pain medication because she hadn't wanted to be impaired in any way when she had to take care of Immy. But she still wondered if something they'd given her in the hospital had come back to haunt her.

That seemed more likely than that Beau Camden could have materialized from the past. At just that moment. And here, of all places.

Yet, as she studied the man outside, she began to see in him small images of the boy she'd once known.

Most definitely in the eyes. Although while the color was the same, the innocence she remembered was lost.

There were also hints of the boy in the features that time had fine-tuned and chiseled, accentuating cheekbones and giving a leaner line to the face that had had more roundness to it fourteen years ago.

At seventeen, Beau Camden had been tall. Maybe not quite as tall as this guy, but close. And his hair had been the same color—though there had been more of it as a teenager that summer.

More hair and far, far smaller muscles…

Still, the longer she looked at him, the easier it was to believe that this was, indeed, Beau Camden.

And with that belief, resentment came back to life.

"Beau…" she said. "What are you doing here?"

"I'm not sure where to start," he said. "Could I come in?"

Had the hospital given her anything that could cause weird flashbacks and hallucinations? Because she just didn't know how this could possibly be happening.

"Are you for real?" she heard herself ask.

He took a wallet from his back pocket, opened it and held his driver's license close enough to the window for her to see it.

It looked new and the picture was exactly of the man standing there. Beaumont Anthony Camden.

Beaumont…

She'd teased him about that that summer…

A good memory all twisted up with bad ones, causing a pain that had nothing to do with the escape from the fire.

"Or it's nice out here—you could come out," he suggested as he put his wallet away.

Since she didn't think hallucinations had driver's licenses, and it began to sink in that he really was who he said he was, she didn't have reason to fear him. He wouldn't hurt her—not physically, anyway. And resentment or no resentment, she was curious about what he was doing there, not to mention how and why.

But she couldn't let him into her room and take the chance that Immy would wake up.

So she said, "Give me a minute and I'll come out."

"Take all the time you need."

Kyla ducked behind the curtains and held them tightly closed in front of her.

Then she opened them just a slit and peeked out again to see if Beau Camden really was out there.

He was. She hadn't imagined this. She wasn't hallucinating.

And he was waiting for her, now standing near a big black SUV parked outside her room. Still posture-perfect, with his long, thick, jeans-encased legs spread shoulder width apart and hands behind his back.

Military for sure.

But now that she knew who he was there was no surprise in that.

She closed the drapes tightly again, suddenly realizing that she didn't know how presentable *she* was.

She went to the mirror over the small bureau near the bathroom.

Once she got there and took a look at herself she thought maybe she shouldn't have.

She'd showered at the hospital that morning, but everything she'd brought with her from Northbridge had been lost in the fire. That meant no makeup, let alone anything to camouflage the dark bruise on her temple or any blush to put color into the pallor that the trauma had left her with.

Luckily there was only one bruise on her face—the rest of her injuries were under her clothes.

Her dark amber eyes weren't blackened or swollen—she counted that as a good thing. Her thin, straight nose was unmarred. And while she wished she had lip gloss, her lips were a natural pink color that hadn't paled along with the rest of her face.

Basically she looked like what she was—someone who had just finished a hospital stay. But there wasn't much she could do about that, so she focused on her hair.

It was about an inch longer than chin length, cut to turn under at the ends, with long bangs that she wore swept to one side. She'd had highlights added to its reddish-brown hue just before leaving home, and neither her hair nor her eyebrows had been singed.

But without her own shampoo and styling products or a curling iron, her hair was lackluster and just hung there limply. The best she could do was brush it with the cheap hairbrush she'd been given and sweep it behind her ears.

Oh, she really *was* pale, she realized. So pale that it made the bruise on her otherwise-unmarred forehead look even worse.

She reached for her bangs automatically with her right hand, forgetting that her wrist was badly sprained until the jolt of pain reminded her.

Then she tried to fluff her bangs with her left hand to cover the bruise. Mostly she just managed to pull them into her face. She wasn't sure that was an improvement, but she left them anyway.

Eddie's secretary had been good enough to get her a few basic necessities that included pajama pants and a top to sleep in, and two pairs of loose-fitting sweatpants to go with two baggy T-shirts for daytime. But that was the extent of her wardrobe. So there was no sense changing out of one pair of sweatpants and T-shirt into the other.

She stepped farther back from the mirror and took a look at the whole picture.

If there was a worse way to look meeting Beau Camden again, she couldn't think of it.

But there was nothing she could do, so she took some small comfort in the thought that if he'd recognized her when she'd poked her head through the curtains maybe she didn't look too different than she had at sixteen.

It was very small comfort, though. Especially when she recalled how fantastic *he* looked…

But she refused to let herself care what he might think—or at least tried not to—as she slid her feet into the flip-flops that were her only shoes and reluctantly headed for the door.

She was careful not to make any noise as she slipped out of the motel room, leaving the door ajar by only an inch in order to be able to hear if Immy cried. And even though it wasn't easy, she made sure she was standing straight and strong before she turned to face her first love and the person who had hurt her more than anyone in her life.

"I have a two-month-old baby sleeping inside and I don't want to wake her," she informed Beau without inflection, staggered all over again by the man he'd become when she looked at him without anything between them.

He gave her a once-over glance that didn't seem to miss a thing—including the bruise on her temple and the wrist brace that went from mid-forearm to her knuckles. "You look like you need to sit. It's finally cooling down today, so how about the hood of my car?"

His SUV was big. Normally she wouldn't have had a problem using the front bumper as a step and climbing onto it. But in her current condition there was no way she could get up there.

"I can give you a hand," Beau offered as if he knew

what she was thinking, holding out that same giant mitt that had pounded on the door earlier.

Okay, sure, there was a part of her that was inclined to slip her hand into his the way she would have that long-ago summer. To see what it was like now.

But it was a very small part of her that was instantly overruled by her sense of independence and her certainty that she would never forgive him for what he'd done.

"No, thanks," she said curtly as she moved to sit on the SUV's bumper. "How is it that you're here?" she asked then.

"There's a lot that goes into that story," he answered, sounding confused and bewildered—something that did not seem in keeping with the powerful tower of man standing before her. "There's a lot—so much—that we need to talk about and I can't even imagine what you must be thinking…what you must have thought about me all these years—"

"Nothing good," she told him without compunction.

"Just let me say that fourteen years ago all I knew was that I'd had an unbelievable summer with an un-believable girl—"

"And then lied about it and left me hanging out to dry with the consequences."

"Honest to God, Kyla, I didn't do either of those things. I didn't even tell anybody about you because I was so wrecked trying to get over you, and I didn't want to be teased about it by my brothers and cousins—I just let them think I was sorry to be home again."

Kyla gazed up at him, but before she could accuse him of lying once more, he said, "We need to talk about it all. But right now isn't the time. Just give me the ben-efit of the doubt when I tell you that, until a few hours ago, I had no idea you'd tried to contact me after the day we said goodbye in Northbridge."

Kyla glared at him.

"Honest to God," he repeated. "And while you certainly don't owe me anything, not even answers, I just have to ask you one thing—do I...do we..."

He seemed to stand even straighter and stiffer than he had been—although she didn't know how that was possible—and she thought he was steeling himself.

"Do we have a kid?" he finally asked quietly.

Kyla didn't want to admit it to herself, but there was an unmistakable tone in his voice that made it sound as if the possibility of that was new to him. Stunningly new to him, shaking this man who appeared to be unshakable.

So she merely answered his question. "No. I...there was a miscarriage—I lost it." And herself for a while.

His expression went blank and he didn't seem to know how to respond.

Then he let out a breath that allowed those broad shoulders of his to relax almost imperceptibly and said, "Okay. Can we put a pin in that, then, and deal with it all later so I can just focus on helping you now?"

"Helping me?" she parroted sarcastically. "*You're* going to help me *now*?" In a week of unfathomable things happening, this was the frosting on the cake. "I don't even know how you got here or why or—"

"My grandmother saw a news report about the fire at your cousin's house. When she heard your name it rang a bell with her because she'd only recently read some things that my great-grandfather wrote in his journal—along with the letter you sent me. The letter I never got." He shook his head as if he'd veered off track and was redirecting himself. "Anyway, your name and the fact that the news said you were from Northbridge caused GiGi—my grandmother—to do some digging. She called my brother Seth—"

"Who runs your ranch in Northbridge now—I know," Kyla said.

"I didn't know you'd gone back there."

Kyla shrugged. She didn't owe him any explanations. He didn't deserve any.

"Do you know my brother?" Beau asked.

"Only by name. We've never been introduced and if he knows who I am—"

"He doesn't. I told you, I never said anything to anyone, so there's no way—"

Kyla wasn't up to arguing this now, so she merely cut him off to say, "No, we don't *know* each other. But Northbridge is Northbridge—everybody at least knows *of* everyone else." And the belief she'd had for as long as she'd been living in Northbridge that his brother was just pretending not to know who she was held fast.

"That's what Seth said—that he knew *of* you. But after GiGi called him he asked around, talked to someone who I guess is your roommate—"

"Darla."

"She confirmed that you came to Denver to visit family, that you *were* in a fire, and she said that the only survivors were you and a baby who's—"

"My cousin's daughter—Immy. My godchild."

"Who's now yours to raise?"

"Rachel and her husband, Eddie, named me as Immy's guardian in their will." They'd told her that. She'd taken it only as another honorary position, not thinking for even a minute that the need to actually *become* Immy's guardian would ever come about.

"And there's a business." He glanced around them.

"These truck stops that you'll need to run until the child grows up and takes over?"

"Three of them, I've been told," Kyla said.

"Your roommate said you don't know anybody else in Denver."

"Eddie's secretary has done a few things for me and she contacted his attorney who came to the hospital, but no, I don't really know anyone…"

"And you're hurt…" He looked her up and down again.

"Not as badly as I could have been," she said.

"But still…how are you taking care of a baby with that?" He nodded at her wrist. "Your fingers are sausages—that can't feel good."

It actually hurt tremendously whenever she had to use any part of her wrist, hand or fingers to do anything with Immy. But she didn't need or want his sympathy, so all she said was, "I manage."

"Here?" he asked, with another glance around that took in the motel and the rest of the truck stop. "On your own?"

He was stating the obvious, so she didn't respond to it.

"Seth said you aren't married, your roommate told him you aren't involved with anyone and don't have any family to come up here to lend a hand—"

"My parents died seven years ago."

"I'm sorry to hear that. And I guess the school year just started in Northbridge, so your roommate has to be there and can't come, either—"

"I teach kindergarten. Darla teaches fifth grade. They got a sub for me, but yes, classes started last Thursday and Darla can't be gone, too."

"So here I am," he concluded. "And I want to help."

He was not going to be her knight in shining armor, if that's what he thought.

"I don't know how you could," she said flatly.

"For starters, this is no place for you and a baby to be staying, let alone recuperating. I have a house—a *big* house—that's more comfortable, not to mention much quieter than this." He nodded toward the sounds emanating from the bustling travel center. "You can have your own room with a private bathroom, and there's another room that the baby can go into. I don't know squat about taking care of a baby—"

"Join the club," Kyla said under her breath.

"—but I'm more able-bodied than you are right now, so I can lend a hand with...what's the baby's name? I know you said it, but—"

"Immogene—but her mom and dad call...*called*... her Immy." Kyla fought a fresh wave of grief at the thought that that was past tense.

"I can lend a hand with Immy," Beau went on, "and you can rest and let me help you get back on your feet. Camden Superstores can provide both of you with everything you need to start over—"

"Darla is just waiting for me to give her an address and she's sending my own things to replace what I lost," Kyla informed.

"Still, I'm sure there are a few things you could use to tide you over, and I'll get the baby outfitted with whatever it is babies need. Then, if you're open to it, when you're better, I can also maybe give you some help with the business side of things, overseeing these truck stops. My own family was left in a situation not too different than this—Camden Incorporated had to be run for a while by people other than Camdens after H.J.

died and before the rest of us were old enough to take it on. *If* you need help with that—maybe you don't..."

A weak, wry, overwhelmed laugh shot out of Kyla and from her muddled emotions came a blurted confession. "I know what to do with five-year-olds, *not* with babies. I don't know anything about being a *single parent*. And when it comes to business...I was raised by people who rarely had two dimes to rub together, and if they did, they squandered them. I definitely don't know the first thing about running any business. And now I have what I'm told is a huge one on my hands. I think Immy might already hate me, and if I'm as bad with finances as my parents were, I could ruin everything Rachel and Eddie left her before she's old enough to *read*, much less take over for herself—"

"So you do need help."

"I don't know what I need," Kyla lamented, fighting the breakdown that she felt on the verge of. But whatever she needed, it couldn't be Beau Camden.

And yet Beau Camden was the only one standing there, offering.

Damn it all, anyway...

Kyla blinked back tears that threatened again, though she couldn't help slumping slightly against the SUV's grille.

"We'll just take it one step at a time," Beau said in a consoling and less stilted voice. "And I'll be there with you the whole way."

It was what he should have said to her fourteen years ago.

And hearing it, Kyla felt the anger and hurt and confusion she'd felt then, surprised that after all this time and even under the current circumstances the feelings could be as strong as they were.

"Please," he said into her negative thoughts, once more as if he could read them. "Let me do this for you now and we'll sort through the past later."

It went against everything in Kyla to accept help from anyone. Ever.

And if she were on her own there was no way she would accept anything from him.

But she had Immy.

And she really was alone in Denver.

Eddie's secretary had been kind, but she was new to the job, barely nineteen, and she already had her hands full dealing with the chaos at the office.

One of the volunteers at the hospital was also a volunteer with the Red Cross and had come to see her. But once the volunteer found out there were resources available to her and Immy through the truck stops Immy now owned, that was the last of the volunteer or the Red Cross.

Eddie's estate attorney had come to the hospital to talk to her and he'd let her know that even though Eddie and Rachel's wills needed to go through probate, he could likely persuade a judge to release funds from the estate for the care and well-being of Immy, as well as for Kyla as Immy's guardian. To tide them over until he accomplished that, he'd advanced her three hundred dollars from his own pocket.

He'd also contacted the truck stop and arranged for their motel room, and for the convenience store and the diner to run tabs for whatever food she ordered and whatever she could use out of the convenience store.

But from there he'd said only that he'd *be in touch*.

The diner food was salty, greasy and very heavy, but more problematically, the one choice of baby formula from the convenience store wasn't the organic stuff

Immy was used to. Kyla thought it was possible that the newborn didn't like it and so was refusing to eat. That potentially had contributed to the problems this evening and could ultimately lead to Immy feeling sick or having digestive ailments.

Kyla's driver's license and credit cards were lost in the fire, so she couldn't rent or drive a car to go outside the truck stop, and she had no idea if taxis were equipped with child car seats to allow her to attempt to get anywhere else.

Plus she didn't even know where she was or where to go from here to try to find Immy the formula Rachel had used.

And besides all of that, Kyla was well aware that she was not only inexperienced and inept with Immy, she also wasn't physically up to caring for the baby altogether on her own. She'd overestimated the strength of her sprained wrist the first time she'd had to lift Immy and nearly dropped her. And even though she was more careful now, using her wrist and hand was still painful and they were very weak.

So while Kyla was inclined to hold her chin high and refuse even an iota of help from Beau, for Immy's sake she didn't think she could look a gift horse in the mouth.

Even if that gift horse was the same person who had left her pregnant and alone with that problem once upon a time.

Still, it meant going to stay at his house. With him…

"Do you have a wife or someone I'd be imposing on?" she asked when that suddenly occurred to her. And made her feel yet another thing she didn't want to feel—a twinge of jealousy.

"No wife. No girlfriend. It's just me," he assured her. "And it wouldn't be an imposition."

"Immy cries and needs to be fed in the middle of the night. And tonight she just cried for a long time for no reason I could figure out," she warned.

"I've been through worse," he said with a hint of the smile she'd never forgotten, a smile that had haunted her. "So what do you say?"

It was galling not to be able to tell him off the way she had in her head many, many times over the years.

But she had to think of Immy. To put her first. And she knew that Immy would be better off if there were two of them to care for her—even two people who didn't know what they were doing seemed better than one, one who was struggling with injuries to boot. And Beau had the use of both hands and a car, so he could go out and find the formula Immy was accustomed to. Plus if they went to his home Immy wouldn't be breathing air polluted with exhaust fumes.

So the bottom line was that Beau's offer was one she just couldn't refuse, Kyla decided. For Immy's sake, if not for her own.

But even as she came to that decision she vowed that the minute—the exact second—she could pack up Immy and handle everything on her own, she'd leave Beau Camden in her dust. Not unlike the way he'd left her.

"Okay," she conceded ungraciously. "But as soon as I get some things in order, we'll be out of your hair."

All he said to that was, "There's a Camden Superstore down the street—I can go there now and get a car seat and whatever else we need and come back—"

The thought of disturbing Immy sent renewed panic through Kyla. "No, not tonight!" she said in a hurry. "You don't know what it took to get Immy to sleep. Tomorrow—we can move tomorrow."

"How about I stay here tonight, then?"

In her room? With her? What was this guy thinking?

Then he said, "The rooms on either side of yours look empty. I can check into one of those, probably hear the baby if she wakes up…"

There would be someone else to see to the baby if the crying started again and wouldn't stop.

It was tempting.

But Kyla shook her head, her independent streak somehow demanding that she draw at least that line. "We'll be all right for tonight," she said with more confidence than she felt. "But Immy *does* have to have a car seat—Eddie's secretary borrowed one to pick us up from the hospital."

"I'll have one by the time I get here—and I'll get here any time you say tomorrow morning. But you're sure you'll be all right tonight?"

She wasn't.

But she also wasn't willing to let him see that. "I'll be fine," she said, hoping she was wrong about Immy not liking the formula she had for her—or at least that the baby would put up with it for now.

"Have you eaten?" he asked.

"I ordered something from the diner. Most of it is still left, if I get hungry."

He nodded and as she watched him do that she thought, *Geez, he's good-looking…*

Then she realized what had gone through her mind and she pushed it out of her head.

"I suppose I should let you go in and get some rest," Beau said then.

Kyla stood, trying not to flinch as she did, and faced him as he took a business card out of his pocket and handed it to her. "My cell phone number is on this. If you need anything—*anything*—just call."

Again, words that were fourteen years too late.

Kyla accepted the card without comment.

"So I guess I'll just see you tomorrow," he said, as if he wasn't sure that was the right course. "What time?"

"Nine maybe…" she suggested aloofly and with no real knowledge of how that would work for Immy. Then she moved to the motel room door again.

"I really—*really*—am sorry, Kyla," Beau said quietly to her back.

Too little, too late, she thought. But all she said was, "Tomorrow," before she went into her room, closing the door on him.

And wondering what incredible twist of fate had put her in the position she was in.

To be rescued by Beau Camden of all people.

Chapter Two

Beau spent the remainder of Tuesday evening on the phone from home causing trouble for several Camden Superstore departments and employees. When he was done, he'd arranged to have his currently unfurnished guest room and a nursery fully outfitted by the time he transported his new charges to his house.

He'd decided it all needed to get underway at zero-five-hundred and to be finished by zero-eight-hundred tomorrow morning.

"Yes, that means the first truck is to be here at five a.m. and the whole job has to be done by eight a.m.," he'd had to explain to more than one person who had acted as if he was out of his mind to believe what he wanted was possible.

But he hadn't brought his men and himself through three deployments to the Middle East by leaving room for error and he wasn't going to start now. This time, unlike the way it had been since he'd been discharged, the civilian world was going to have to adjust to him rather than the other way around.

Since going to the den with GiGi that afternoon and learning what he'd learned, he'd been on Marine autopilot. Show no emotion. Stoic composure at all costs. Do whatever it took to get the job done and make sure everyone under his command knew the same thing applied to them.

As one of the ten owners and board members of Camden Incorporated, everyone who worked for Camden Superstores was basically under his command. It was something he'd verified with Cade before taking action.

By then word had already circulated within the family about what was going on with him, so he hadn't had to explain anything. Instead Cade had reminded him that everything the family owned and everyone they employed were at his disposal. Cade had told him to do whatever was required, and had given him the names and numbers of the people to contact.

"Anything you need, however many people you need to get it done," he'd been told. *"We're all still spinning over this one involving you...I'm sorry, man..."*

"Yeah, me, too," Beau had said emotionlessly before going on to take charge.

He doubted his inflexibility had made him any friends among Camden Superstores employees tonight. Because tonight he'd pulled rank and his orders weren't going to be easy to follow.

Not that he cared. This was top priority, even if decorators didn't ordinarily arrive at their offices until nine or work so fast, even if items weren't usually delivered and set up before ten. Tomorrow it all would be. At least here it would.

But as Tuesday ticked into Wednesday there was no more he could do. He was finally off duty. At home. Alone.

He'd poured himself a short Scotch when he'd returned from that truck stop tonight and come into the den to get busy. Most of the drink was still left in the glass on the desk he was sitting behind. He reached for it and finished it in one gulp.

The next thing he knew he'd thrown that glass against the wall, shattering it into a million pieces.

Then he took the first deep breath he'd taken since reading the entry in H.J.'s journal and exhaled until it felt as if his lungs had collapsed.

Yes, the military had trained him well not to show emotions during the course of a mission.

But nothing could keep him from having them.

Especially not these.

And now that he was off duty, they rose to the surface.

To Beau the wrongs that were done in the name of building Camden Incorporated were disgraceful. It was still a struggle to resolve the fact that those actions had been taken by men he'd loved and respected. Men he'd known were strong-willed and determined—like any good marine—but men he'd believed were honest and decent, too.

But the knowledge of what they'd done to other people was bad enough. He didn't know how to process that his own life had been screwed with by one of H.J.'s conspiracies.

Or what to do with the emotions that knowledge had let loose in him.

He'd thought there was nothing worse than learning that the men in his own family had, in reality, no honor to them. And he'd fully supported the family's plan to make amends.

In fact, wanting to do that had contributed to his decision to come out of the service now.

He'd told GiGi that she could give all of the projects to him from here on, that he was volunteering for that duty. That he was willing to make it his own personal undertaking to atone on behalf of the family.

His grandmother's response had been odd. She'd gone too quiet and very pale. She hadn't seemed to be able to make eye contact with him. But he'd taken her excuse that he needed time to get his land legs back at face value.

Now he knew what had really been going through her mind. She'd already read the part of the journals that revealed what had been done to him and was just waiting for him to settle in before she broke the news to him. She'd already known what was unimaginable to Beau—that he was one of the people H.J. had wronged.

Along with Kyla.

And potentially their baby.

Because if Kyla had lost that baby out of stress, or by doing something dangerous or foolhardy in hopes of ending what she didn't want to deal with on her own, that made that loss H.J.'s fault, too, as far as Beau was concerned.

No, he definitely didn't know what to do with how it all made him feel...

He'd brought Kyla's letter with him into the den and it was in front of him. He read it for about the tenth time since his grandmother had given it to him today.

Kyla had written it only weeks after he'd left the ranch that summer.

When he was home again, starting his senior year of high school. Being patted on the back and congratulated on his official candidacy for admission to the naval academy at Annapolis.

Not everyone had known because he'd received the news in June, after school was out. The news had been the reason he'd opted to spend the summer in Northbridge. Once he knew for sure Annapolis was where he was headed, he'd wanted to start toughening up for the military by doing ranch work.

He'd accomplished that—gaining some muscle mass and stamina.

But he'd also met Kyla Gibson...

Today was the first time he'd seen the letter. The first time he had any knowledge whatsoever that Kyla had changed her mind about the end of that summer being the end of any contact they had with each other.

In the letter—the letter addressed to him—she told him that she was pregnant. That she'd just found out. She said she didn't know what to do. She said she hadn't told her parents yet. She said she hoped that Beau would have some idea of where to go from there. That he'd get hold of her, maybe come back to Northbridge for a weekend so they could figure something out.

Holding that letter in his hands, staring at the words written on the page, Beau could see the hope she'd had that he would offer some solution, some help, some support, anything that would tell her that she wasn't in it alone.

And again emotions rose that he could hardly stand.

H.J. had written in his journal that he'd intercepted the letter. He'd visited the ranch a few times that summer. He'd seen Beau with the daughter of one of that summer's hired hands. He'd seen how unhappy Beau was when he'd come home and had put two and two together, figuring that Beau was in the throes of his first love.

But that summer was over and—according to H.J.— the romance needed to be, too, so that Beau wouldn't endanger his future.

H.J. wrote that when he'd seen the Northbridge postmark and the return address with Kyla's name on it, he'd decided it couldn't contain anything that would do Beau any good. Better a clean cut with the girl—that was what H.J. had written at the time.

He hadn't even opened the letter. He'd just tucked it away.

He'd only learned about the pregnancy when Kyla's father had shown up on the doorstep two weeks later.

Which was when H.J. took the second step in keeping Beau from knowing about Kyla's situation.

"It's a good thing you're not here now, old man," he threatened from between clenched teeth.

Yes, going to Annapolis had been what Beau wanted from the day his great-grandfather had explained to him that that was the best course into the Marines. And, yes, a teenage pregnancy, a child, would have canceled his candidacy and the full acceptance that was contingent only on his graduation.

And yes, that would have crushed a part of him.

But even then, even before becoming a marine, Beau had had a marine's mentality. Honor, courage and commitment—those were the words he'd stenciled over his bed when he'd read that they were the core values that defined a marine. He'd been eleven. And from that moment on they were his values.

Sure, it would have taken courage and stamina to endure losing his opportunity to go to Annapolis. Courage to face all of his family with news that he'd gotten a girl pregnant.

But he would have done it. And he would have honored his responsibility to that girl and to that baby. He would have made the commitment to them that needed to have been made. He would have taken the responsibility that was his.

If he had known, he would never—ever—have abandoned Kyla.

And not only because of those Marine Corps values.

The truth that he alone knew was that he probably would have viewed it all as an excuse to do what he was fighting not to do every day at that same time—get on a bus back to her and Northbridge.

He was seventeen. Flooded with hormones. And a beautiful, smart, funny girl had, suddenly that summer, become what he wanted as much as he wanted to be a marine.

He'd been so in love with Kyla that he hadn't been able to see straight and he'd physically ached to get back to her.

It had taken the will of a marine to get him to choose, each day, *not* to turn his back on everything he'd ever been about and just get himself to wherever she was.

If he'd been handed that letter then, if he'd opened it and read it, nothing would have kept him away from her.

It would have been his sign from the universe that he was meant to change his course. Because that was what he'd been wondering at the time—if meeting Kyla had been a fork in the road that fate had created because maybe he was meant to choose her instead...

Hell, even as a marine, every time he'd been in a

situation that he might not have come out of alive, he'd wondered if maybe he was supposed to have chosen Kyla and a life with her over a life in the service.

But his great-grandfather hadn't had any doubt about what choice was to be made.

So Beau had become a marine.

And Kyla had lost the baby.

And gained every reason to think he was the scum of the earth.

That twisted him up inside.

Over the years he'd never forgotten her. She—and that summer with her—were some of his best memories.

Whenever he'd thought of her, he'd wondered what had happened to her, where she was, what she was doing. A couple of times he'd told himself that if he came out alive he was going to look her up. He'd fantasized that when he did she wouldn't be married or have kids and maybe they'd click all over again.

So much for that.

Although something *had* clicked for him...

When he'd wondered about her he'd also wondered if she would still look the same, and she did. Better, actually, even bruised and clearly weary and unwell and dressed in sweats that were too big for the body that had rounded only in the right places.

The spark and the glimmer were still in those honey-colored eyes that weren't like any others he'd ever seen—the dark amber of the beer he liked.

Except for that bad bruise on her temple, her skin was flawless now, with not a single imperfection to distract from lips that were just full enough to make them outrageously kissable. From high, apple-round cheeks that had always had a natural blush to them and made her look as though the sun hadn't been able to resist kissing her, either. A natural blush that anger had tried to bring back tonight, so he was confident it had only been lost temporarily.

She hadn't smiled at him earlier, but even so he'd been able to see the hint of the dimples that would appear when she did. Tonight they had only been small indentations that reminded him of what they could become. Of the way they made every smile beam. And how much he'd liked bringing them out.

Her hair was still the same color—reddish-brown, silky and shiny. But she wore it differently than she had when they were teenagers. Now it was shorter and it framed her face—and since it was a face so worth framing, he liked it. He also liked the section that had fallen over that bruise—it added a little spice to that girl-next-door look of hers.

She was just a beautiful woman, blossomed from the beautiful girl she'd been.

And his very first instinct when she'd stepped out of that motel room door had been to wrap his arms around her and hold her so tight she couldn't get away again.

So, yeah, something had clicked for him.

And why, of all the things that he needed to be fitting into place, that was the one that had, he didn't understand.

For two months now he'd been struggling to get something to feel right. He was like a fish out of water in civilian life. Everything seemed so unorganized. So inefficient. So undisciplined. People were lax. Too much was at ease too much of the time.

He sure as hell didn't feel as if he was on the same wavelength as his family. They were trying hard. He was trying hard. Maybe they were all trying *too* hard. But either way, he felt like an outsider. A stranger. He didn't know what they were talking about most of the time and he didn't feel as if he had anything to contribute himself.

He hadn't found a position he wanted in the business. Everything was running perfectly well without him, and board meetings pretty much went the same way family social events did—he didn't know what the issues were and he certainly didn't feel as if he should interrupt what was already running smoothly by putting his two cents' worth in.

He was just failing at reacclimating all the way around.

And then tonight...

Seeing Kyla again was the first time since he'd taken off the uniform and put on civvies that something had clicked.

It was probably just some kind of throwback to the past. After all, they didn't really know each other—not the people they'd grown up to be.

And Kyla had had years to hate him after only a few months when things had been good between them. She'd had fourteen years to live with *her* reality—that he'd left her pregnant and alone to deal with it rather than stepping up, taking his share of the blame and responsibility, and doing the right thing by her. Fourteen years with every reason to hate his guts and for that to have taken deep, deep root. To be ingrained in her.

Which made things a whole lot different than they had been that summer.

But nothing changed the mission, and he told himself to keep his goal in sight, to maintain his focus.

The mission was to make amends by helping her, and that's what he was going to do.

And if, in the process, it provided him with a temporary distraction from all his failures to assimilate, and he got the chance to let her know that he wasn't some lowlife who had turned his back on her or on his baby and his responsibilities to them both, the mission would be a complete success.

But as for the clicking?

That was nothing.

That was an emotional component and he knew what to do with it—ignore it. Keep it in check. Proceed as if it didn't exist.

Which was exactly what he would do.

Kyla jolted awake at the soft knock on the motel room door at the stroke of 9:00 a.m. She was sleeping sitting up in a chair.

Not that she'd intended to fall asleep. The chair was near the room's window and she'd been watching for Beau.

She'd been up with Immy four times during the night. Four times when Immy had again been unhappy, crying and refusing to take much formula.

And even when the baby had finally gone back to sleep and Kyla had been able to return to bed herself, she'd had trouble dozing off again. Thinking about Beau, about the past, and trying to figure out any way she could refuse his services had kept her up even more than Immy had.

Unfortunately she'd arrived at the same conclusion each and every time—for Immy's sake she had to accept Beau Camden's help. Temporarily.

And now that was upon her.

Stiffly, she pushed herself out of the chair and went to open the motel room door.

She'd been hoping that he might have looked better

in the darkness last night than he would in the stark light of day. Instead the reverse was true and summer sunshine just emphasized how incredibly handsome he'd grown up to be. And one glance at him instantly thwarted her best intentions not to notice it.

Freshly showered, his strikingly angular face cleanly shaven, dressed in jeans and a simple white crew-neck T-shirt that hugged each and every one of his finely honed muscles, it wasn't humanly possible not to notice that he was one very, very hot man.

"Hi," he greeted her, sounding tentative.

"Hi," she responded with resignation and no warmth whatsoever.

"Bad night?" he guessed after giving her the once-over.

Just what every girl wanted to think—that it showed. Especially when she was facing a drop-dead-gorgeous guy.

"Pretty bad," she confirmed without going into detail. Poor Immy was going to get the full blame because Kyla wasn't about to let him know he'd contributed to her sleeplessness.

He peered over her head at the crib inside the room. "Is she asleep now?"

"For a little while. It won't last—she isn't eating. I think she needs the formula she's used to instead of what I have."

"We'll stop and get some on the way," Beau was quick to assure her, as if her wish was his command. "I've got a state-of-the-art car seat ready and waiting, belted in by people who knew how to do it the right way, in the backseat. Think we can move her into it without waking her up?"

Kyla shrugged. "Rachel and Eddie could pull it off

sometimes. I know I can't—I'm really clumsy when it comes to lifting her with this wrist."

"I'll give it a try. Let me load up your stuff first. Why don't you sit down again and—"

"There's just this," she said, pointing to the white plastic trash bag beside the door. "That's everything."

"Okay." He reached in and grabbed it, taking it to the rear of the SUV and depositing it there. Then he opened the door behind the driver's seat—apparently that's where the car seat was—and leaving the door open, he returned to her.

"The guy who set up the car seat talked me through where the belts and straps go. If I just get her into it I think I have that part straight. How hurt is she?"

"The doctors and nurses said she isn't injured at all. I've been worried about it, but I haven't seen any sign that it hurts her to pick her up or hold her or change her diaper or anything. I…" This was going to sound crazy. "I actually rolled her in bubble wrap to get out of the fire and I guess it helped. The hospital was mostly worried about her lungs—from the smoke. But as of yesterday her lungs got a clean bill of health, too. And the way she's been exercising them, I'd have to say that they're fine."

"Bubble wrap?" he repeated, almost cracking a smile.

Stuck on the crazy part. That figured.

"I had it to wrap a pitcher I was going to take home to Darla, so it was right there and…I just rolled Immy in it—everything but her face—in case I dropped her or something, then I wrapped another blanket around the bubble wrap and out we went…"

"Fast thinking," he said as if that was something he approved of.

"That happens when the place is on fire and the roof is caving in," she said, deflecting his approval.

He nodded. "So it won't hurt her to pick her up?"

"It doesn't seem to, no."

"And…like I said, I don't have any experience with babies… Do I just scoop her up?" he asked, demonstrating by holding out both of his hands, palms up, and thrusting them forward.

"She's not hurt, but she's kind of delicate just because she's only eight weeks old," Kyla warned, alarmed by the force in his demonstration. "You have to be careful with her—one hand under her head, neck and shoulders to support them, the other under her rear end."

"Got it."

Kyla felt less confident than he sounded, but she made way for him to come into the room and followed him to the crib, mentally willing the infant to stay asleep. And Beau not to drop her.

She kept an eagle eye on him, but unlike his bravado at the door, he was infinitely cautious when he actually reached for Immy. In fact, he went at a snail's pace, easing his big hands under her and raising her from the mattress as if she were a bomb that might go off at the slightest jarring.

Which actually wasn't far from the truth, in Kyla's experience.

But this time Immy didn't so much as whimper even as Beau straightened up and pulled her close to—though not completely against—his flat belly.

It was awkward and not pretty, but from the sight of his bulging biceps and forearms it was a weight he could bear without bracing her against him, so Kyla didn't say anything.

He gave Kyla an almost imperceptible shrug and nod

that said he guessed he'd pulled it off, and took the baby out to the car, with Kyla again following close behind.

Immy went on sleeping like an angel as he laid her very gently in the car seat that had a soft, fleecy head support at the ready. Then he strapped the infant in and closed the door firmly but without slamming it.

"Okay," he said, as if the first of many steps had been accomplished. "Now you."

"I can take care of myself," she assured him curtly, returning to the motel room to close the door.

Still, Beau was waiting, standing sentry-straight with the passenger door open for her when she turned back to the SUV.

"It's a pretty high step up—you should let me help you," he said, holding out his hand to her.

There was no way Kyla was accepting it.

"I'm fine," she said, gritting her teeth to hide the pain it caused her to get into that seat on her own and hating that she was less than graceful doing it. But she still made it and managed the seat belt with her left hand only.

Beau's expression was completely blank when she caught sight of his face, so she had no idea what he thought of her stubbornness or her lack of agility—or if he'd even registered any of it. But once she was belted in he closed her door the same way he had Immy's.

Who remained asleep through Beau getting into the car, too, and starting the engine.

Kyla had already called the front desk to let them know she was leaving, so there was no need for anything but to get on the road.

As Beau merged onto the highway, Kyla took note of too much about him. More even than how great-looking he was. The SUV was big and yet she couldn't see him in anything smaller. Not only had he bulked up considerably, but he exuded so much power and presence that it just seemed to take a large space to accommodate it. He was like a brick wall of man—a force to be reckoned with. Quite a change from when they were teenagers.

He also smelled fabulous—a clean, citrusy scent that gave him an added appeal to go with how mind-blowingly handsome he was now. Altogether it made for a heady mix that was getting to her. A little.

Until she reminded herself that fourteen years ago he'd lied about what had happened between them and denied it all.

Until she reminded herself that he'd portrayed her as some kind of slut.

And abandoned her.

That steeled her against his current appeal.

"How did all this happen?" Beau asked then, nodding at her braced wrist.

Small talk. Okay.

Kyla explained how and why she'd come to Denver, the housing situation on her cousin's property, and how she'd come to have Immy with her that night.

Then she said, "The fire department thinks it was an electrical fire that started on the second floor, where Rachel and Eddie's bedroom was. I was asleep in the guesthouse. There was no smoke alarm—I'm not sure what woke me up, but whatever did, it was already too late for me to do anything but get us out. I could see the main house through one window and it was… Mostly I could just see huge, bright flames. And the guesthouse was on fire, too—there were flames right outside the bedroom door, and I guess the roof out there fell in, because there was a huge crash. I just kept thinking that no one would know we were back there in the guesthouse, to come and help, and I had to get us out."

The terror of that memory flooded Kyla.

"I slammed the bedroom door to keep the flames out—I was just hoping that if the fire had to burn through the door it would give me a few more minutes. Luckily Immy was in a portable crib in my room—if she'd been anywhere else I wouldn't have been able to get to her. But the only way out was the window in the bathroom that faced the back. We were above the garage and…" Kyla swallowed hard and shrugged. "I didn't really know what to do. I thought about throwing Immy out first, but I was afraid to do that. Like I said before, the bubble wrap was right there, so I rolled her in it, wrapped a blanket around that, and—"

"Jumped out the window?"

"It was really more like we fell out the window—I kind of got us up to sit in it. It was a straight drop from there. I tried to hold Immy to one side and twist so I'd fall on my back and maybe be the cushion for her. But I ended up falling on my other side—Immy was on my left and I fell on the right—and I guess maybe I tried to brace us or catch us or something with my hand out." She shook her head. "I don't know for sure—that part is a blur—but the next thing I knew I was on the ground and Immy was crying and I was hurt and it was so hot, and I knew I needed to get us to where someone would be able to see us to help because we were way in the back."

She shrugged again. "I got over to the neighbor's place next door and out to their front yard. Somebody saw us coming then and…there was help, but I couldn't find Rachel or Eddie, and I kept asking where they were. I think I just kind of collapsed."

Beau took his eyes off the road for only a second. "You did a lot before that—you'd make a good soldier."

Kyla shook her head. "No, thanks."

"How long was it before you knew that your cousin and her husband hadn't made it out of the fire?"

"I'm not sure of that, either. My concept of time from there is off. I know I started to think it was bad when no one would tell me anything about them. I kept asking—the EMTs in the ambulance, the hospital staff—but all anyone would say was that it was Immy and me who they needed to think about. Immy was in the hospital nursery and they kept me informed about her, but it was sometime the next day I think when they finally told me Rachel and Eddie hadn't made it."

Kyla had to blink away tears at that thought, and as she did she focused on the scenery to get herself out of the nightmare in her head.

They'd driven into the heart of Denver and now they seemed to be in an area called Cherry Creek, where the houses were old and enormous.

Beau pulled into the driveway of a beautiful, stately two-story white Colonial saltbox with wings that stretched out from both sides of the first floor. It was trimmed in black with wood shingles, there were two chimneys on the roof, and lantern sconces on either side of a red front door.

"*This* is your house?" Kyla said, amazed by the difference between it and anywhere she'd ever lived.

"It has been for three weeks."

"For only three weeks—are you still living out of boxes?"

"No, ma'am," he answered as if that could only be true of a slacker. "There are some empty rooms—two less as of this morning when one got turned into a nursery and another into a guest room—but you'll find it shipshape."

"And you live in this huge place alone?"

"Yes. When I'm left alone," he said, nodding in the direction of a sedan parked at the curb as he pulled farther up the drive. There was a woman sitting behind the wheel.

"That would be my sister January," he explained. "Jani, we call her. Uninvited, but with good intentions, I'm sure. I've only been back for two months—"

"Back?"

"Out of the Marines, back to civilian life. And things are...we're all trying to figure out where I fit in with the family again. The females in particular seem to hover and try to take care of me as if I need that."

He sighed as if to maintain patience that was strained. "Anyway, I'm betting Jani is only the first platoon to be sent in today and the rest will just 'happen to stop by.' I'm sorry. I didn't ask for their help, but brace for it, because it's likely to be coming at us today."

Kyla tried to grasp this newest twist as he followed the curve of the drive around the west wing to the attached garage that was hidden behind it. As he pulled in, something seemed to suddenly occur to him.

"I forgot to stop for formula!"

Without Immy crying, Kyla had forgotten about it, too.

"Okay, how about this," he said as the garage door began to close behind them. "Since the baby is still sleeping and she's safe in here, we'll leave her where she is while I get you in and settled, with the car door and the door into the house open so I can hear her if she wakes up. And we can send Jani for formula."

"Sure. Okay," Kyla agreed vaguely as a whole new stress took over.

Because now his family was entering the picture.

People who believed that once upon a time she had falsely accused Beau of fathering her baby. How would they react to seeing her suddenly in Beau's life again—and with a baby in tow?

Chapter Three

Oh, Darla, thank you, thank you, thank you! Kyla thought as she washed her hair with her own shampoo late Thursday afternoon.

Within an hour of arriving at Beau Camden's house the day before, she'd called her Northbridge roommate with his address. Darla had an entire box of Kyla's own clothes, toiletries and necessities waiting and had mailed it overnight. She'd even included some new things—like a hair dryer and curling iron—to replace what Kyla had brought with her to Denver and lost in the fire.

The box had been delivered an hour ago and just having her own belongings again was more of a boon than Kyla would ever have guessed. Despite the bumps and bruises and still-bad wrist, it made her feel worlds better.

Although the way she'd spent the time since getting here had helped a lot, too.

Beau had been completely correct when he'd said that his sister Jani's visit was only the beginning. She'd been joined within half an hour by the family's grandmother—who Kyla had been instructed to call GiGi—and GiGi's private physician.

The doctor had consulted with the hospital staff that had treated Kyla and Immy, so he was familiar with their conditions. He hadn't liked the toll taken on either of them by the motel stay or the lack of sleep and food, and had ordered Kyla to another twenty-four hours of bed rest.

At that point what Kyla had assumed would be a short visit from Beau's family had actually become full-time care by the Camden women.

Jani and GiGi had set her up in the enormous guest room, on a queen-size bed with a heavenly mattress and sheets like nothing Kyla had ever felt. And afterward she'd been waited on hand and foot by a stream of female members of the Camden family.

Jani and GiGi and Beau's cousins Lindie and Livi had taken turns caring for her—complete with meals served to her in bed—right up to the time Kyla was ready to sleep for the night. Lindie had even spent the night in the nursery to look after Immy and had been there for Kyla again when Kyla woke up this morning. Once she was awake, the shifts had begun again.

Each and every one of the Camden women had been incredibly warm, kind and friendly, squelching Kyla's worries that they thought badly of her. But as of this afternoon the additional twenty-four hours of bed rest was up. And because she felt better than she had since the fire, and because she never accepted anything from anyone that she didn't absolutely need, Kyla had thanked

GiGi for everything and assured the elderly woman that she could take over from here.

She hoped even as she did it that Immy wouldn't pay too dearly for Kyla's independent streak. In the Camden women's hands the infant had finally become as content as she had been with Rachel and Eddie—something Kyla wasn't confident she would ever be able to accomplish herself. But regardless of her own fears about dealing with Immy, Immy was her responsibility.

Plus Kyla had seen neither hide nor hair of Beau since the Camden women had stepped in, and while she told herself that suited her just fine, it also made her slightly suspicious.

Had he had a change of heart about having her here and secretly enlisted the help of his family so he didn't have to deal with her?

It was possible. After all, there was a precedent set for her believing one thing about him and then him proving her wrong and running out on her. If he'd changed his mind she needed to know about it, Kyla decided as she finished her shower and stepped out of the stall.

There was a warming lamp overhead and the towel she used was also heated. Like the room and the bedding, the towel was the height of luxury—huge, thick and fluffy—and it struck her that fourteen years ago, when she'd first laid eyes on Beau working under the hot Montana sun out in a field, she'd had no idea this was his lifestyle.

Yes, she'd been aware that he was part of the family that owned the ranch, the family that owned Camden Superstores, but she hadn't had any real concept of what that meant. He'd just been a cute guy her own age who flirted with her.

At least, that was how it had started.

For some reason, as she gratefully put on her own underwear and struggled through several attempts to hook her bra, it was the young Beau Camden who was on her mind.

Her parents had been free spirits who had wanted desperately to have a career in music, and they'd taken Kyla along on their nomadic pursuit of that. Living out of a mobile home or in cheap apartments wherever they landed for more than a weekend, her parents had haunted music festivals and fairs all over the country, performing and attempting to sell the recordings they'd made of themselves. Always with the hope that they'd be discovered.

The longest the small family had stayed in any one place was when they went to cities where the music industry offered opportunities. Then her parents worked whatever jobs they could get while they knocked on doors and tried every ploy to get auditions or convince the bigwigs to listen to their demos.

But when nothing panned out in one place, after a while they'd go back to making the rounds of the fairs and festivals until they could afford another move to the next music industry hub.

It was a music festival in Northbridge that took them to Montana that summer. The plan had been to work during the week and spend weekends at several other fairs and events scheduled in that area of the country. Kyla's father had taken work on the Camden ranch because it offered free housing and the use of a small portion of land on which they could grow vegetables for Kyla and her mother to sell at a roadside stand.

Without any intentions of staying for long, neither Kevin nor Lila had bothered making friends, and by then Kyla had learned not to put too much effort into it, either. Plus, since it was summer vacation and she wasn't in school, and since they were living outside town, Kyla simply hadn't had the chance to connect with anyone.

Anyone but Beau, who was also spending the summer on the ranch.

No boy should have eyes that blue—that's what she'd thought the first time she'd met him.

Or a smile as good as his. She still remembered the moment when he saw her, took her in and seemed to give his approval with that cocky, self-assured grin. It had lit sparks in her blood and made her want to take him down a few pegs at the same time.

Which she'd done by ignoring his every attempt to draw her attention and impress her.

In fact, she'd let him think she couldn't remember his name for a week. And then she'd given him a terrible time over that, too, calling him *Beaumont* for the second week. But underneath it all he'd really been getting to her, and suddenly a summer that had seemed as if it would be endlessly boring had put on a new suit. Every day she hadn't been able to wait for the chance to see him.

The teenage Beau hadn't been anything like any other boy she'd ever met. Strong, steadfast and sure of his path in life, he was also so cute she couldn't take her eyes off him. By the end of that June she'd just wanted to be with him every minute of every day and night.

The same way he'd wanted to be with her.

So when he'd told her he loved her it wasn't something she'd doubted for a minute. Any more than she'd doubted that she loved him.

Until her father had come back from Denver to tell

her Beau's response to her pregnancy. From then on those words had just seemed like a rich boy's ploy to get what he wanted.

That thought soured the sweeter memories as Kyla worked to pull on a pair of jeans and a plain blue T-shirt one-handed, and it strengthened her determination to leave if he'd changed his mind about helping her now.

Yes, she could see the value of being here rather than at the truck stop motel, the value of having help taking care of Immy. But she would never accept reluctant hospitality if that's what it had turned out to be. Especially not from Beau Camden of all people.

There was a dressing table in one corner of her room and she went to sit at it, opening the cosmetic bag Darla had sent her and peering into the mirror on the wall.

The bruise on her temple was dark purple and impossible to cover, so she stuck with mascara and blush—difficult enough to apply with her left hand.

Then she wielded the large-barreled curling iron—also with her left hand—to turn the ends of her hair under.

When she brushed it, it fell into her normal style and she was glad to see that she could accomplish that, at least, without the use of her right hand.

She was still pale beneath the blush and had that ugly bruise, but at least if her hair wasn't flat and limp she looked a little more like herself. And looking more like herself helped her feel slightly less at a disadvantage with the hunk that Beau had grown up to be.

And why did he have to go and do that? she thought.

Why couldn't he have grown into some skinny, weasely man the way he deserved for leaving her pregnant and alone? Why did he have to be not only good-looking, but *incredibly* good-looking?

If someone did something truly awful it should be reflected in their appearance in some way, shouldn't it?

Certainly they shouldn't end up being big and strong and rich and powerful and hotter than a lit match.

Darla had sent her a few choices in footwear and she opted for a pair of sandals she could slide her feet into without much trouble. Then she went out of the bedroom for the first time since she'd gotten there.

There was no sign of anyone on the second floor.

She went to the nursery beside her room and opened the door slowly to poke her head in and make sure Immy was still napping.

Jani—who was pregnant and had formed an instant attachment to Immy—had been there before Kyla's shower to feed the baby and put her down for a nap. Kyla wasn't sure if Jani had left after that. She hoped so. She hoped that she would go downstairs and find Beau alone so she could figure out right away if he really didn't want to be bothered with her or Immy.

Since Immy was sound asleep with no one else in the room, Kyla went on to the top of the stairs.

But she stopped short there. They led down to a large entryway with the house's main door directly in front of the staircase. Looking down now she could see Beau standing in the open doorway. She couldn't see beyond him, but she heard him say, "No, Lindie," so she assumed that was who he was facing out on the porch.

Then he went on in a don't-question-my-orders tone of voice. "I'm telling you all—no more! I heard the shower upstairs a while ago and as long as Kyla can do that on her own, I can do everything else. I brought her here so I could take care of her and that baby, and that's what I'm going to do!"

So he *hadn't* changed his mind.

That was more of a relief to Kyla than she wanted it to be.

She couldn't hear what Lindie said, but Beau's frustrated response was, "Yes, I know the baby needs a bath. I'll take care of it. But that's it from you guys. Done! Finished! Thanks, but no more! I can take it from here!"

Kyla wasn't sure if she should retreat or intrude and ended up just standing there. Lost all of a sudden in the view of Beau from behind.

How could she not be? She wasn't blind and his backside was as much a work of art as his front side was. Those shoulders were something! And the biceps peeking from beneath the ragged edges of cut-off sweatshirt sleeves were enough to make any woman's mouth water.

"I appreciate that you all want to help," Beau said then, regaining Kyla's attention. "I know you're all worried that I can't handle this. But I can. And if I run into anything I *can't* handle, I'll call."

His cousin must have accepted his decree because goodbyes seemed to be exchanged then and Beau closed the front door.

At the sound of it clicking firmly shut, and before he'd turned away from it, he said, "Can I figure that if you still wanted them all around, you would have stopped me?"

Is he talking to me? Kyla wondered in a small panic. How did he know she was up there eavesdropping? She hadn't made a sound, there was nothing that would reflect her image and he hadn't turned around.

But he did just then, turning and glancing up at her without any surprise that she was there, as if he'd known it all along.

"Do you have eyes in the back of your head?" she asked.

"Combat," he said as if that was an answer. "Helps keep you alive to be as aware of what's going on behind you as you are of what's going on in front of you."

Not only a marine until two months ago, but apparently in a war zone.

Kyla mentally filed away what she was learning about him and headed down the steps, belatedly answering his question. "The twenty-four hours of bed rest is over," she said. "It was nice of everyone to do what they've been doing and I appreciated it, but—"

"They were hovering," he concluded as she reached the bottom.

The breadth of his chest provided quite a canvas for the sweatshirt with the letters USMC stenciled on the front. And even dressed in hanging-around-the-house clothes, his face was still cleanly shaven and there didn't seem to be anything about him that was relaxed.

"They *were* hovering a little," she conceded. "Like you said yesterday, they meant well. And I feel a lot better after everything they did, so I'm not complaining. But no, they don't need to go to the trouble anymore."

Those bright blue eyes of his gave her the once over, settling on her face in a way that seemed to bring a sort of softening to them before he said, "You look better... like you *feel* better," he amended. "How's the wrist?" he asked then. "Your fingers are still sausages."

"Bed rest didn't do much for that. Maybe you should have let Lindie stay to give Immy a bath..."

"No," he vetoed instantly. "I did some research, watched a video on the internet and believe me when I tell you that we are now well-stocked with every baby gadget known to man. My grandmother and sister and cousins have had me out running around since they took you upstairs—every time one of them showed up they'd thought of something else we should have and they sent me out for it."

"I hope you kept receipts so I can reimburse you—"

He frowned as if she was talking nonsense and merely continued with what he'd been saying.

"I've stocked up on some kind of clothes called *onesies* and diapers and bottles and some deal that bounces her or sways her or rocks her or…I don't know, maybe it shoots her to the moon, too. I've got a thing that goes in the sink to give her a bath and towels with hoods shaped like animals and baby body wash and…you name it, they've sent me out for it. It takes less gear to send men into battle, so we should have whatever we need."

Kyla shrugged. "Rachel had a lot of stuff, but I didn't pay any attention to it. It's probably good that they all know what's necessary."

"They're getting ready for Jani's baby, so they know everything—"

That came out sounding as if he was calling them know-it-alls and apparently he heard it, too, because he took a breath and sighed, amending his tone. "Don't get me wrong—I love them and I appreciate that they care so much and want to help. But the fussing gets to me."

She could see that.

"So," he said then, as if getting down to business. "If you're up to it, why don't you let me give you the tour so you know your way around. *Are* you up to it?"

"Sure."

Jani had ushered her upstairs immediately the day before, so all Kyla had seen of the place was the route Jani had taken her on from the kitchen to her room and the nursery.

The guest room and nursery were beautifully decorated, warm and cozy. But outside of them the second floor had no adornment whatsoever—no family photographs on the walls, no artwork, nothing in the alcove where a cute little table or desk could be, not even cushions in the two window seats of the dormers she'd seen.

Kyla hadn't thought too much about it until he began to show her around the first floor. The house was larger than anything Kyla had ever been in, which gave the impression of luxury. But spacious room after spacious room contained only a bare minimum of furnishings, all arranged for pure functionality without a single decoration or any personal touch to make the house a home.

"The guest room and the nursery are a lot different from the rest of the place," she ventured when the tour was complete and they ended up in the kitchen where only a coffeemaker and toaster adorned the white marble countertops.

"I had one of the decorators from the store do those," he informed her, without adding whether or not he intended to have them do more to the rest of the house later on.

And she didn't feel free to ask.

"Can I get you something to eat or drink?" he said then.

"I don't need to be waited on. If you show me where the glasses are I'll get myself some water."

"Glasses are here," he answered succinctly, opening a cupboard near the huge side-by-side refrigerator-freezer. "Water and ice can be had from the front of the fridge. Feel free to help yourself to whatever's inside."

Kyla fought the smile that threatened at that. His instructions were clipped and cursory and she was beginning to feel like a new recruit being shown the barracks.

"Pantry is here," he continued, moving to a portion of white bead-board wall.

The kitchen had a country feel to it despite its lack of decoration and—like the rest of the house—had so many possibilities for warmth and charm that weren't being emphasized.

"You just push…" Beau said, demonstrating by giving a framed section of the wall a shove that moved it inward and then opened that portion of paneling that was really a door.

Just out of curiosity, Kyla peered into the walk-in pantry, finding only two shelves with anything on them—everything lined up neatly.

"Bread, chips, nuts, cereal, protein bars, cookies—anything you want, have."

Sir, yes, sir…

The words went automatically through her mind just as the baby monitor on the counter suddenly transmitted the sound of Immy's waking-up noises. Beau snapped into action.

"I'll get her. Have your water and sit, rest."

"Yes, sir," Kyla said, the words escaping this time on their own.

Beau seemed to catch himself, screwing that handsome face into a grimace for a moment before he said, "Sorry. My family keeps telling me to lighten up. I'm not good at it yet."

Kyla merely nodded as Immy began to cry in earnest and he headed in the direction of the stairs.

She'd barely gotten her water and perched on one end of the bench seat that went with the large U-shaped breakfast nook before he was back, with Immy in one arm and a stack of baby things in the other.

"What do you think? Bottle then bath, or bath then bottle?" he asked, clearly hitting on the first thing he wasn't certain of since he'd blocked Lindie at the front door.

"I'm not really sure," Kyla confessed, trying to remember what Rachel had done. "I guess I didn't pay much attention to a schedule—if there was one. Now that I think of it, sometimes Immy just woke up for a bottle and went back to sleep, and other times she was awake for a while and then had a bottle right before they put her to bed. She isn't crying…seems like bottles are for that."

"When she was up this time yesterday Jani didn't feed her right away. She walked her around the house and took her outside, then…I don't know, she put her on a blanket on the floor and did some kind of coo-cooing thing for a while."

"Then bath first," Kyla guessed without any authority.

"Okay, bath first. I'll do it, but you'd better make sure the water is the right temperature." He dropped the stack of baby things on the counter, then glanced from Immy back to it all. "And maybe you could hold her while I get set up."

Kyla joined him and he passed Immy to her. Though once she was holding the baby in her left arm, it wasn't easy to turn on the water and test it with her injured right hand.

Beau realized that as he covered the counter beside the sink with the towel and stepped in. "Should I take her back while you do the water?" he asked.

"No…maybe just turn it on and start to fill the sink and I can test it."

"Okay," he said, doing as she'd suggested.

How could two intelligent, educated people be so stumped by this? Kyla wondered as Beau filled the sink and she repeatedly poked the tips of her swollen fingers into the water until it was warm enough but not too hot.

By then Beau seemed to have arranged everything he'd brought with him in some sort of order—including a foam insert he'd put into the sink—and he was putting his huge hand into a pink bunny mitt as if it was a driving glove.

Kyla couldn't help laughing and it brought a perplexed frown from Beau.

"What? It's like a spongy washcloth. It was with all the other bath stuff."

"It's very cute," Kyla said in the midst of another laugh. "Rachel just put some soap in her hand, but that's another way to go."

"It's really soft," he said defensively. "My hands might be too rough otherwise."

"Okay," Kyla said even as she laughed yet again. "It's nice that you thought of that. It's just…it doesn't go with the rest of you."

He used the mitt to splash a little of the bathwater her way. "Don't give me any guff. You're no better at this than I am," he countered, this time in a tone that was only playfully stern, one she remembered well. He'd used it whenever she'd teased him when they were kids.

But they weren't kids and Kyla reminded herself not to let down her guard.

Beau reached for Immy then. "Okay, I'm ready for her. Give her to me and go sit down again."

Kyla held Immy just enough away from her body so he could take the infant from her without touching her. But once he had Immy on the counter she ignored the rest of his orders and stayed by his side just in case.

Despite her fears, he didn't do too badly with the bath on his own. Once Immy nearly slipped out of his grip and Kyla lunged to catch her, but he corrected the situation before the baby's head went under water and before Kyla could do anything with her one good hand anyway.

Kyla talked him through diapering Immy when the bath was finished and Kyla had patted her dry. They fumbled through dressing her in a pair of footed pajamas like the ones Rachel had favored, then Kyla told Beau about swaddling—something Rachel had taught her—and they both breathed a sigh of relief at having accomplished what seemed like a feat.

The remainder of the afternoon and early evening centered on Immy, and opening and assembling the equipment Beau had purchased for her—an abundance of things stacked in a corner of the family room.

That busywork succeeded at keeping Kyla in the present and warding off thoughts of the past, which helped stave off her resentment.

It lasted through Immy's feeding, through Immy's burping, through Immy falling asleep and right up until Beau stood to take Immy to bed.

But that was when he looked pointedly at Kyla and said, "How about if we order a pizza for our own dinner and maybe talk about…things?"

Kyla knew what he meant by *things*.

And that was when the past and present collided once again…

"Will you tell me your side of the story?" Beau asked.

Even after he'd taken Immy to bed they'd still skirted the subject of their past. They'd discussed pizza toppings, where in the house to eat, whether to use paper plates or not, what to drink.

But now that the pizza had been delivered and they were sitting opposite each other in the breakfast nook eating, Beau brought it up again.

"My side of the story?" Kyla said, her voice instantly gaining an edge it hadn't had earlier. "I realized I was pregnant not too long after you left Northbridge that summer. I didn't know how to get hold of you—"

"Because you said it was useless for us to try to keep in touch. You didn't have a cell phone of your own and your parents could barely afford theirs, so you weren't allowed to get calls on it. You said that you never knew where your family would go next, that even once you got to wherever that was, you'd only have internet access away from home..."

She had said all of that because it was true. And while it had been hard—and oh-so-painful—she'd had to be realistic. She'd wanted more than anything to believe they might be able to keep up a long-distance romance, but she'd known through her history of constantly moving around that trying to maintain even friendships just didn't happen. That once she was gone, she was forgotten, and that when she tried to reconnect she was just left facing that fact.

It was a thought she hadn't been able to bear when it came to Beau.

So yes, she had put up a brave front, and said her goodbyes intending them to be permanent. They hadn't exchanged so much as an email address.

"I did say that," she admitted. "Then I had to get your family's Denver address from the guy who was running the ranch."

"Which is where you sent the letter I just got the day before yesterday."

"Lost in the mail all these years?" she questioned bitingly.

He shook his head. "Intercepted by my great-grandfather and tucked into one of several journals that my brother Seth found not long ago. GiGi has been reading them and she found the letter. H.J. wrote about what he did, but I want to hear your side."

Pizza didn't go down well with all Kyla was feeling, so she wasn't eating much of it.

"I sent the letter," she said. "When I didn't get any answer, I had to tell my parents on my own."

Beau wasn't eating much better than she was, and at that his eyebrows rose and his voice got quiet. "How was that?"

"Awful! A pregnant sixteen-year-old daughter, a *grand*child, medical bills and another mouth to feed? None of that was in their plans, and we were short on money already. It was the maddest they ever got at me."

And the most afraid she'd ever been—crazy, irrationally scared that they might just go on to the next stop without her.

But pride wouldn't let her say that to him.

"I told them I'd written to you to tell you," she went on. "But that I hadn't heard from you. That made them even madder. So my father decided he was going to Denver to deal with you and your family. That this wasn't going to be just *our* problem."

"And that's what he did. He came to Denver."

"Yes, as you know perfectly well because you saw him here."

"I never saw your father again after I left Northbridge. It was H.J. he met up with when he got here," Beau said.

"You did too see him!" Kyla's voice raised on its own. "My dad said H. J. Camden himself called you in and you swore you'd never touched me! That if I was pregnant, there was no way it was yours! Like I was some kind of skank who could have been with anybody! Who *had* been with *everybody*!"

The words flooded out with all the anger that had been festering for fourteen years.

"Oh, Kyla, that just didn't happen. It wouldn't have happened. I wouldn't have done that to you."

He wasn't shouting. He was calm and he even made that sound genuine. But Kyla wasn't buying it.

"My dad said you admitted we'd spent a lot of time together but swore it was only as friends—as if there wasn't anything else you *could* be with the daughter of the hired help! And your great-grandfather believed it and backed you up!"

Beau shook his head in unwavering denial.

But Kyla didn't waver, either.

"My dad said that H. J. Camden threatened to bring his lawyers into it if we tried to push for any help or support from you. He said he'd fight us tooth and nail. That we'd have to get a court order for even a paternity test. That he'd make sure my name was smeared long before yours ever was because he wasn't letting anything or anyone hurt your chances of going to Annapolis when you graduated. My dad said H.J. swore he'd crush us like bugs and that you just stood by..."

Beau shook his head again. "I don't know if H.J. made those threats or not—he could have. I wasn't there and he didn't write about that. I do know that he wouldn't let anything keep me out of Annapolis."

"So my dad said there was nothing we could do. That H. J. Camden could ruin all of our lives and we couldn't afford to fight him. I had to accept that you were out of the picture and never try to contact you again."

Beau didn't flinch. "And were your parents still mad?" he asked.

There was something suggestive in his tone—a hint that the question was leading somewhere.

"No," she admitted tentatively, wondering what he was getting at. "My parents got a lot more understanding after that. I figured they knew I hadn't been with anyone but you all summer and that they felt sorry for me because of what you'd done."

She'd thought that they'd finally come to see that she'd really loved him and was devastated to have him deny her.

"After that they were supportive," she went on. "They said it was my decision what to do—whether to have the baby or have an abortion. That they were with me either way, but they didn't want to see my life ruined."

"So there was pressure for an abortion."

He said it as statement of fact, as if he already knew that.

"They thought it would be for the best." And just remembering that, remembering the way she'd felt, made her eyes sting with tears she was not about to let fall.

"Had you decided when you miscarried?" Beau asked then.

"No, I hadn't decided. I didn't know what to do…" Because there had been a part of her that had wanted their baby. That had wanted to keep that part of him in spite of everything. And she'd hated herself for it.

"Then the decision was taken out of my hands," she concluded, reliving for a moment how sad that had made her. Relieved but so, so sad, too. Reliving the depression she'd sunk into for a long while because she was so despondent over losing him and their baby.

They'd both stopped eating altogether by then, but Kyla took a drink of her iced tea to wash back the tears that still stung her throat and eyes.

Then she took a deep breath for strength. "Now you want to tell me your side," she accused, her tone uglier than she'd intended it to be.

He let that lie for a moment and she wasn't sure if he was weighing his words or hoping the pause might diffuse some of her anger.

Then, in a voice that was deep, very solemn, and quiet again, he reiterated, "I was *not* there the day your dad came to Denver. I never saw him. I never saw your letter. I never knew anything about the pregnancy. If I had, I'd have gotten to you—come hell or high water, Kyla, Annapolis or not—I'd have gotten to you. I was pretty messed up over you at the time as it was—that would have given me the reason I was looking for."

He'd been looking for a reason to get back to her?

That sounded good. But if it was the truth, if he'd wanted to get back to her—pregnancy or not—he knew she would be in Northbridge for a while after he left, so it would have been easy for him. And he hadn't come back.

Kyla just raised a challenging chin at him, saying nothing.

"In his journal H.J. wrote that he made a deal with your dad," Beau went on then. "H.J. paid him a chunk of money—a big chunk—to make the *problem* go away. I have the canceled check, with your father's endorsement on the back. It was with your letter in the journal. I can show it to you—"

Kyla swallowed hard and shook her head, not wanting to believe what he was saying.

"And I wouldn't *ever* have said or implied that you were a skank," he added. "No one in the family knew anything except H.J. If GiGi had, she would never have stood for me not doing—"

"Don't say 'doing the right thing,'" Kyla cut him off. "I hate that. It makes the father sound like some kind of hero, handing out a favor."

"That isn't how it would have been, either. If I had known..." He shook his head. "Everything would have been different. I was so broken up over you. It wouldn't have mattered what anybody else said or thought, I would have gotten to you. I'm telling you, it would have given me the reason I was looking for," he insisted.

"But H.J. knew that," Beau continued. "He wrote that he knew I was *lovesick*—his word. He was worried that I was going to do something *stupid* over you. He wrote that when he heard you were pregnant, he knew that if I found out I'd forget about Annapolis. He wouldn't let that happen. And burying problems under a whole lot of cash was one of the ways he took care of things— he paid people off."

Kyla wanted to throw that notion back in Beau's face. To shout that there was no way her parents would have done anything like that.

But she knew better.

Certainly until right then the thought that her father had taken H. J. Camden's money hadn't occurred to her. Not for one single minute.

But now...

She didn't have to see the check made out to her father or his signature endorsing it to put two and two together. There were other things.

It wasn't only her parents' fury at her that had changed after that trip to Denver. It wasn't only that they'd been more sympathetic and understanding. When she'd miscarried not long after her father came back, her parents had announced that they were finally going to try their luck in Los Angeles.

Los Angeles had long been their goal, but the cost of living in the larger music meccas like New York and Chicago and Nashville had been financially disastrous for them. Before her father's trip to Denver they'd said they were a long, long way from being able to try LA.

But not only had they suddenly been able to afford that, once they were there they'd also had the money for better housing than they'd been in before, and more elaborate and expensive attempts to launch their music career.

Kyla had wondered about it at the time. But she'd been sunk in her own misery, fighting to recover physically and emotionally. So she hadn't delved too deeply into the vague reasons her parents had given her when she'd asked.

She'd never known exactly how much money her parents had available at any given time. And she'd thought that—in their own way—they were trying to cheer her up by going to LA, by getting a nicer place than usual, because that's what they'd said.

But now that she knew this, money from H. J. Camden was a far more likely explanation.

Her parents had profited from her pain.

That wasn't an easy thought to have.

But there hadn't been much about growing up raised by Kevin and Lila Gibson that had been easy for Kyla.

"So that's where the money came from," she said, her voice so low it was barely audible.

"You knew about the money?"

"No. Well…there were some things I didn't understand, things we hadn't been able to have or do before because we couldn't afford it. But when I asked they said there was an end-of-summer bonus from the ranch, and that the roadside vegetable stand had brought in more than they expected. I was…kind of a mess myself," she said. "I just took what they said at face value."

Beau was silent, leaving her with her own knowledge of her parents and the past.

Kyla was grateful that he didn't say anything insulting or offensive about her parents, that he left her what little pride in them she had left.

But it *was* a lot to take in and she wasn't sure how long she sat there, staring at the oak tabletop, remembering more and more things that this information explained. Trying not to feel angry at two people who were long gone, at what they'd done so many years ago. Wondering a little why it surprised her that they would have done something like this.

"You really didn't know?" she asked then, wishing her voice hadn't come out so small. But since she honestly hadn't known what had really gone on, it made it more difficult to insist that he had.

"I really didn't know," he said sincerely. "If I had I would never—*never*—have let you deal with any of it without me."

She could see that being true of the man he was today. But what about the boy?

It had been so hard then to believe that he'd denied their being together. So hard to believe that when he'd said he loved her he'd merely been trying to get what he wanted. So hard to believe that he wasn't the person she'd thought he was. But she'd come to believe it. And now to reverse that belief…

But these pieces were the pieces that really fit. That really made sense.

"I'm sorry, Kyla," Beau apologized to her again. "If that old man was around today I think I'd wring his neck."

Kyla acknowledged that sentiment by raising her chin. "I guess at least you can say that what your great-grandfather did was in your best interests. What my parents did was just…selfish."

"None of them had the right to make the decisions for us, no matter how young we were."

He was angry. It was under control, but Kyla could see the fury in the clench of his jaw.

And out of everything, that went the furthest in convincing her that he really hadn't known anything at the time.

"I suppose it's all water under the bridge…" she said then.

"For me it's fresher than that."

That was an odd twist, Kyla realized. While she was struggling with long-held and deep-seated angers and resentments, this was all new to him and so were the angers and resentments. It almost made her want to apologize to him, though she wasn't sure for what.

So instead she said, "I wouldn't have wanted to be responsible for keeping you from going to Annapolis, becoming a marine—you'd dreamed about that from when you were a little boy." She knew that because he'd talked so much about it.

"Still, what they did was wrong," he said with conviction.

There was no arguing with that, so she didn't try. And as strange as it seemed for her to say it and mean it, she said, "Maybe we just have to put it behind us."

He raised those blue eyes to her, his brow furrowed above them. "Can you do that?"

That was a good question.

She couldn't very well go on resenting Beau or being angry with him for something he hadn't done, could she?

All she could say was, "I can try," because she also knew that it might take a little while for the truth to alter feelings she'd carried around for over a decade.

He nodded as if he understood that and she appreciated that he didn't try to force instant forgiveness, that he was accepting blame he wasn't due.

There was a quiet strength in that that she couldn't help admiring.

Some of that same strength she'd seen in him fourteen years ago, strength that had set him apart. That had drawn her to him and made her like him.

And she had liked him.

So much...

She looked at him then and for some reason remembered the first time he'd kissed her.

She hadn't kissed many boys before him because she'd never been in any one place long enough to have a real boyfriend. But Beau had seemed to have more experience—when it came to kissing, at least.

They'd been on the pier. His arm had been around her shoulders. And he'd just swiveled from the waist toward her and kissed her...

The best kiss she'd had up until then.

And one she'd never forgotten. Not even when she'd wished she could.

Okay, enough, she told herself. She'd had too much for one day—being out of bed and active, all the Immy stuff, all the talk of the past and everything that had stirred up—she was on overload and her brain was launching things at her that she was not at all equipped to handle.

"We didn't do much justice to this pizza, but I think I need to call it a day." She just had to get away, to be alone with everything she'd learned, to get some control over her wandering thoughts.

Beau didn't try to stop her. Instead he nodded as if he thought her calling it a day was a good idea. "Go on up. And leave the baby monitor—I'll take care of Immy through the night so you can get some rest."

"In the middle of the night it's just a diaper change, a bottle and a burp, and she should go right back down," Kyla instructed. "At least, that's the ideal. If you have any problems—"

"I'll scream louder than she does."

There was just the faint hint of a smile to let Kyla know he was joking.

She smiled back the same way, her gaze catching on that sexy mouth of his.

And those thoughts of kissing him flew back at her until she dodged them by sliding out of the breakfast nook and getting to her feet.

"Barring you screaming in the night, then, I guess I'll see you in the morning," she said.

"If you need anything—"

"I'll be fine."

She only made it a few steps away from the nook when his deep voice sounded again.

"Kyla?"

She stopped and peered at his way-too-handsome face over her shoulder.

"I really am sorry," he apologized yet again.

Only this time her answer was, "Me, too."

Then she left him sitting in the kitchen, feeling his eyes on her the whole way out.

And once more she struggled against the invasion of those thoughts of long-ago kissing.

Against wondering what it might be like to kiss him again now.

But in the struggle she also made it clear to herself that she was never going to know.

They were a long way away from those days when they used to kiss, and she didn't see them going back— not as the very different people they were now.

There just wasn't anything in their future but the time it took for her to get on her feet and figure out her game plan.

Then they would part ways again.

And nowhere in that was there going to be kissing.

Chapter Four

Zero-hundred this. Zero-hundred that.

Kyla only partially listened to Beau over breakfast on Friday. Her head was still swimming with all he'd revealed to her the night before about what had really happened fourteen years ago.

After so long condemning him she found herself in some kind of no-man's-land with the whole thing. She couldn't say that she'd forgiven him because if he'd been kept in the dark about the pregnancy there wasn't anything to forgive him for.

She guessed that she was on the road to accepting that, at least—that he honestly hadn't even known that she was pregnant and so hadn't abandoned her or denied her or said terrible things about her.

And that was something. Not resenting him was something...

There was more of the zero-hundred talk and she told herself she needed to concentrate.

They were sitting in the nook in his kitchen eating cereal. Immy was content in the infant seat, being mechanically swayed back and forth between them while Beau outlined the schedule he usually kept, the schedule he thought Immy should be on—based on research he'd done on the internet—and the schedule for the most efficient and effective rest and recuperation for Kyla.

She had no idea how the military time jargon translated into hours and minutes, but it caused her to think that if there was such a thing as over-organization, Beau Camden had the market cornered.

At least, that was what she was thinking when she wasn't thinking about the past or the way his gray USMC T-shirt fitted him like a second skin, or how great his rear end had looked in the jeans he was wearing when he'd bent over to put Immy in her chair.

"That should take us right up to when the lawyer will be here this afternoon," he seemed to conclude.

"Wait…did you say the lawyer?" Not surprisingly, she'd missed something.

"Your lawyer—I told you he called when you were still upstairs this morning."

"Right. Sure," she said as if she'd known all along.

She'd given Beau's number to Eddie and Rachel's lawyer after moving in—she just hadn't expected to hear from him so soon.

"He said he has something to talk to you about," Beau reminded. "He'll be here at seventeen-hundred, after he leaves his office for the day. Immy woke up at sixteen-forty-five yesterday, so that would give us just enough time for a diaper change, but if we don't do her bath until just before bedtime tonight—the way the website advised—we should be okay. Let's say an hour and a half with the lawyer, then bath, bottle, bed-time and—"

"Okay...wow..." Kyla said. "First off, I don't under-stand military time, so could you put me on real time?"

"Sorry, I keep doing that..."

"And I agree that trying to keep Immy on a sched-ule is good—Rachel did that. But you have to be a lit-tle flexible, too. She's a baby, not an alarm clock, and sometimes things vary a little, so you probably shouldn't think any schedule can be followed to the minute—she might sleep half an hour longer or get up earlier—"

"But the closer a schedule is followed the better," he said, not allowing for much of that flexibility she'd mentioned.

"And I appreciate that you've worked out that I should nap when Immy does," Kyla went on, "but I don't really like to nap. Even in the hospital and here for that last day of bed rest, I didn't sleep during the day. I'm not operating at full speed right now and I can tell when I need to sit down and take it easy, but to sched-ule it doesn't really work for me."

"But you *will* rest."

He just didn't budge, did he?

"Sure," Kyla conceded. "If and when I need to. But I'm not an invalid. I feel better today than I did yester-day and I think that's the course I'm on now—every day I'll be a little better. Some of the swelling has even gone down in my fingers and I can almost start to bend them..."

She demonstrated, though her ability to bend her fingers was still minimal and painful.

"And actually," she continued, "I like to be busy." What she was really thinking was that she didn't want to just sit around and look at Beau all day. She needed her attention *not* to be so much on him because every time he was within her line of vision she lapsed into studying him and noticing all over again how hot he was.

And she didn't want to do that. Even when she succeeded at resolving the resentment she'd felt all these years, it still wasn't as if there was or could be anything between them. They might have hit it off when they were teenagers isolated on a small-town ranch, but that wasn't what they were any more. Now not only weren't they teenagers, they'd grown up to be very, very different people who tackled things in very, very different ways with very, very different drives for control and regimentation.

So the last thing she needed was to be cataloging assets and appeals that didn't ultimately matter.

"I'll do as much as I can with Immy," she informed him. "And I can make formula and fill bottles—I just have trouble screwing on the nipples."

Ooo…had that sounded to him the way it had to her? Because to her it had sounded sort of racy.

She couldn't tell if he'd reacted. His expression was always so emotionless that it was indecipherable.

So she merely continued. "And if there's anything I can do around here to earn my keep, I'd like to do it. Like if you want a woman's touch decorating, or maybe you have some family photos I could help you hang, or maybe there's a box of knickknacks you're just waiting to find a place for to add some personal touches—"

"You don't like the house."

"It's a beautiful house. But you just moved in, right? You're only starting to decorate and put your own stamp on it." That seemed like the most diplomatic way to address it. "The guest room and Immy's room are warm and homey—maybe you're just waiting for whoever decorated those to do the rest?"

"I didn't have any plans for that, no."

"Then maybe when Immy is napping this morning and this afternoon, we could do a little of it ourselves to make the place feel like your own, if you want. Or if there's something else I can do…" Though she didn't know what because it wasn't as if there was a speck of dust or a crumb on a counter or a single thing out of place. And she *did* only have the use of one hand, to make matters worse—giving advice was close to the extent of what she was capable of.

He stared at her for a while, his expression still showing nothing. She hoped he was considering her offer and not that she'd offended him, but she did some damage control anyway. "I'm just trying to find a way to be useful. Maybe your decorating style is just the clean and spare look…"

"I'm pretty sure I don't have a *decorating style*," he admitted, two slight lines pulling his brows together to let her know that in this—if not in much else—he wasn't so sure of himself and the way everything should be done. "Jani and my cousins keep telling me I have to do *something*—get a decorator or let them do it. They say the place doesn't look like anybody really lives here. They've brought stuff—for the walls, stuff I guess you'd call knickknacks. I don't know what to do with them— if things don't have a useful purpose, I don't really see the point. But everything is in one of the rooms upstairs. I guess, if you want to take a look—"

"And you know there are ways to arrange furniture that aren't just lining everything up along a wall like it's all at attention," she ventured since she thought she might be on a roll. At least he seemed open to the suggestion.

"Yeah, I don't get that, either. But hey, have at it—if you're sure you're up to it and you let me do the work and you tell me when you need a rest."

More rules that put him in command again. He just couldn't stop.

And she couldn't resist a flippant salute.

"Oh, that is *all* wrong," he said and this time it was the fact that just one side of his mouth quirked up in a slight smile that gave her a sign that somewhere behind all the muscle and marine might be a flicker of the guy she used to know.

"I will rest if I need to," she assured him. But to prove her point about *his* needing to be more flexible she nodded toward Immy who was now sound asleep in her chair. "But your schedule is already going to be off because she isn't supposed to be doing that yet, right?"

He glanced at the sleeping infant, then raised perplexed eyebrows at her and said, "Now what? Do we put her in bed and risk that she wakes up? Or let her sleep in that thing and risk that she won't nap long enough because she isn't in her bed?"

Kyla laughed, more happy than she should have been just to see some emotion on his face. "Oh, come on, Answer Man, you mean you don't know?"

"Do you?" he challenged.

"No," she admitted with another laugh.

And just like that Kyla thought she could feel the air around them change. The air that had been so tense it had felt heavy between them since he'd shown up at the motel.

Maybe she was closer to letting go of the past than

she'd realized, and without the old baggage things *could* lighten up between them.

"Shall we flip a coin?" Beau suggested.

"That seems like as good a way to decide as any," she agreed.

He dug a quarter out of his jeans pocket. "Heads we leave her. Tails I put her in her crib."

"Okay."

He flipped the coin, but Kyla's eyes followed his big, capable hands rather than it.

"Tails," he announced. "Guess she goes upstairs."

"I'll clear this while you do that," Kyla said. "And before you say it—" because she saw it coming "—I can take two bowls and two spoons to the sink, rinse them and put them in the dishwasher without falling down dead from overexertion. Then I'll meet you upstairs to have a look at your secret stash of knickknacks."

"Okay, whatever you say," Beau said as he sat down with Kyla at the dining room table to wait for the attorney. The two of them had spent the day working on the house. But despite his efforts to keep his tone agreeable, he seemed no more convinced now than he had been before that it was necessary. "I'm just not sure what the point is—a table is for eating at or putting your feet up on or holding a glass while you watch TV. Sticking one somewhere just for the look of it doesn't make sense to me."

Kyla had found a wealth of treasures in the unoccupied bedroom upstairs that he was temporarily using for storage. Apparently his sister and female cousins had been trying to move him in the direction of decorating since he'd purchased the house.

Kyla felt as if she'd succeeded where they'd failed because while Beau remained skeptical, he had accepted all of her suggestions that he use everything. As well as those about rearranging the furniture.

In the process Kyla had learned two things about him—that he took orders well even from her, and that he also had an amazing amount of pure brute strength and stamina.

He'd moved massive pieces of furniture on his own and could hold the heaviest objects on a wall longer than anyone she'd ever seen. And he did it without complaint. So apparently not all of the leftovers of his military service were bad.

He also had finely tuned hearing because he heard the lawyer's car pull into the driveway when Kyla hadn't registered anything at all. He got up to answer the door before the bell had even rung, leaving Kyla and Immy behind.

Immy was contentedly sucking on her fist in her bouncy chair on the floor, and after a glance at her, Kyla looked up into the mirror she'd had Beau hang on the wall across from the table.

She was feeling more worn out than she'd been willing to admit to Beau, and she was wondering if there were visible signs of it.

There were—not even the blush she'd applied that morning was concealing her renewed pallor.

But there was nothing she could do about it now. Pale and dressed in a filmy white V-neck T-shirt over a white tank top and a pair of black knit workout pants was what the lawyer was getting because she'd also been too weary to change clothes.

Still, when Beau ushered the business-suit-clad David Cannary into the dining room, the attorney said,

"You're looking better than when I saw you at the hospital."

She knew that, at least, was true, so she thanked him and assured him she was feeling better.

Beau offered him the seat at the head of the table and asked if he could bring him something to drink.

The lawyer declined and got right to business, explaining that he had papers Kyla needed to sign accepting guardianship of Immy.

Of course she'd known it was coming. But the formality of that rocked her. Especially when he went on to tell her that she might want to consider going through adoption proceedings in order to become Immy's mother rather than merely her guardian.

Kyla just kept thinking, *But Rachel is Immy's mother, not me...*

Except that Kyla *was* Immy's mother now.

And the weight of that sat heavily on her all over again.

"Are you okay?"

It was Beau's deep voice that cut through her thoughts.

She caught sight of herself in the mirror and saw what Beau had apparently seen—she was even more pale than she had been and she had the look of a deer caught in headlights.

But it wasn't as if she *wasn't* going to accept guardianship or possibly adopting Immy in time, so to Beau—as if she hadn't just been struck by it all over again—she said, "I'm just a little tired."

Then she signed where David Cannary told her on the guardianship papers and told him that she'd think about adoption.

From there he moved on to telling her that he'd succeeded in getting funds released from Rachel and Eddie's estate and explained how Kyla could go about accessing them.

Then he told her that an offer to buy the truck stops had come in from a national chain of similar travel centers.

"The memorial service isn't even until tomorrow," Kyla said in surprise and with a hint of outrage. "And someone is already—"

"The truck stops are very successful—Eddie even bought additional land and had plans underway to build two more in the next three years. It's not uncommon for feelers to be put out right away if something happens and it seems that a business like this might come up for grabs," the lawyer said in a mollifying way before he went on to outline the offer.

And not only did Kyla find herself buried under the emotional impact of formally accepting responsibility for Immy, she got lost listening to things she didn't understand for the second time today—these things far more important than Beau's scheduling suggestions.

"Okay...just—wait!" she said when she felt a little like she was drowning. "I know about hand puppets and the cleanup song and how to recognize the first signs of attention deficit disorder in five-year-olds. But none of this makes any sense to me. Between military time this morning and this now—"

"Do you mind if I ask a few things?" Beau asked her.

He was rescuing her. She could see it. Feel it. And even though it irked her to admit she might need it, she said, "Be my guest."

From then until early into the evening, she tried to ride along on Beau's coattails as he explored details of both the business and the buyout offer. There wasn't a lick of it that she understood and the longer it went on, the dumber she felt.

So she was glad when David Cannary summed up and spoke more directly to her again. "That's all I can tell you for now. And I can't advise you one way or another, to sell or not to, but like I said, this is a lowball offer. So at the very least I would recommend some negotiation on Immy's behalf to raise the price."

And then do what with so much money? Kyla thought.

But she didn't say that. Between being completely overwhelmed again and already having admitted that her business knowledge was lacking, she wasn't about to bring up a third thing that she felt ill-equipped to deal with—a vast sum of money that would need to be protected and invested.

So she merely said, "I guess I'll have to think a lot of things over..."

"There's no rush," the lawyer assured her. "And if you have any questions about anything, I'm always just a phone call away."

Kyla thanked him for that and said goodbye before Beau showed him out, leaving her alone with enormous feelings of inadequacy.

She was holding Immy—halfway through the meeting the baby had gotten fussy, and Kyla had taken her so Beau could concentrate on the business meeting without the distraction. Now she glanced down at the infant who was sucking wildly on a pacifier and shook her head. "I really, really hope I don't screw things up for you," she said to her new charge.

"You won't," came a deep-voiced reassurance from the dining room's doorway before Kyla had realized Beau was back.

"Ah, you're stealthy, too," she said, sounding as defeated as she felt and also adding yet another thing to what she was learning about him.

"Training," he said.

He crossed to her and took Immy out of her arms. "You've had it today," he decreed then. "Pick a spot to land while I give Immy her bath and feed her and get her to bed. GiGi came by this morning just after dawn with our dinner—I'll put that in the oven to heat so it'll be ready when I'm finished. But you're done."

She was tempted to salute him again, but it had occurred to her since the last time that that might be offensive to someone like him who took everything—and certainly everything military—ultraseriously. So she resisted and just confessed, "I *am* sort of tired. Maybe I'll just go upstairs and figure out what to wear to the memorial service tomorrow."

"Good idea. I'll call you when it's time to eat."

"You're sure?" she asked with a glance at Immy.

"Yes, ma'am."

Something about that made her laugh. "Isn't that just the frosting on the cake of the last two hours—now I'm a *ma'am*."

"Well, you're not a sir," he said with another hint of that one-sided smile.

And why that made her feel better, somehow, all on its own, she had no idea. But it did.

She bent over and kissed Immy on the forehead, bidding her good-night before she headed out of the kitchen.

Then she remembered that Beau had been worried about judging the water temperature for the baby's bath the day before and she turned to address that.

Catching him in the act of looking unmistakably at her rear end.

With a very readable expression on his face that said he was appreciating the sight.

Before he snapped his eyes up and the soldier stoicism replaced it.

Kyla fought not to smile. Or to be flattered by his ogling and appreciation.

She also opted not to say anything, instead addressing only what she'd turned to tell him in the first place.

"When Eddie gave Immy a bath he tested the temperature of the water with his elbow because he said his hands were too tough, too."

"I'll do that then," Beau responded before she left.

But nothing could take away the secret pleasure of knowing that she wasn't the only one of them doing a little subtle rubbernecking today.

Even if neither of them should have.

"Okay, the baby's down for the count, we've had dinner, the kitchen is clean and here we are, finished with the decorating now, too," Beau said to Kyla when all of that was indeed accomplished and they were in his den.

Kyla hadn't quite completed arranging things there that afternoon, so they'd returned to it after dinner. She was sitting in one of the two wingback chairs, testing the positioning after having him move them from across the room to face his desk. He was sitting on the desk, one leg hooked over a corner of it in front of her.

"And you still seem a little dazed. Are you all right?" he asked.

"No," she said, as if it went without saying.

"Are you feeling sicker again or is this fallout from today?"

"Fallout," she said emphatically. "I just can't get a hold of all this—being a *parent*, and a figurehead truck-stop mogul, and a manager of big, big money… I don't know if I'm up to any of it."

"You're getting the hang of Immy."

"Barely. And don't get me wrong, I love her and I promised my cousin I would do this and I will. But—"

"I get it—just the thought that I might have a kid out in the world hit me like a grenade."

There was something about his understanding that opened the door to her unloading on him—her worries about how she was going to be able to juggle the job she loved and didn't want to leave because of her sudden single parenthood. Her worries about how she could possibly do both of those things as well as run the truck stops. About how she didn't know if she'd be making an enormous mistake to sell them or an even bigger mistake not to. About how she didn't have the slightest idea how to manage either the business or the kind of money involved if she sold out.

"After the way I grew up I just wanted a little structure. I wanted to make a home for myself—in one place—and stay there. I wanted to go to the same job every day in a workplace that was bright and cheery and fun and friendly. I wanted to see the same faces from one week to the next. To have friends. My parents wanted a big life that they never got. I wanted a small one. Small and plain and simple. And I *did* get it! That's how it's been since I moved to Northbridge. But now nothing is small or plain or simple!" she said as all of her fears rushed out.

"No, it isn't," Beau confirmed.

"My little savings account is the extent of me managing money," Kyla went on. "Running a roadside vegetable stand or a booth at a flea market or peddling my parents' recordings at music festivals is the closest I've

ever been to business. What if I just wreck everything?
What if Immy grows up a mess with nothing of what
her parents wanted her to have waiting for her—all because of me?"

Beau nodded. "I get that, too," he said, as if he genuinely did. "My life has changed and it isn't easy."

Kyla had only been thinking about herself, but she
suddenly realized that yes, it *was* true for him, too. He
was just out of the military after years and years. And
she'd sort of made fun of those lingering military aspects of him rather than being sensitive to why he might
cling to them. Plus she'd pushed him about the house
when maybe he'd wanted the place to look like military
living quarters because it made him feel better.

"Do you want to put the knickknacks and useless
tables and lamps and mirrors and things back in the
room upstairs and push all the furniture against the
walls where you had it?" she asked contritely.

He laughed.

It was such a good sound.

And his gorgeous blue eyes lit up and crinkled
slightly at the corners.

And that lush mouth of his spread wide and gloriously and showed off perfect white teeth.

And for no reason it made her warm all over just to
see it, to hear it.

"Why would I want to *undecorate*?" he asked.

"I pushed you into it. You might have liked it better
the other way because it was so…because it reminded
you of where you've been for the last thirteen years."

He shook his head, still smiling a small smile that
helped maintain the warmth she'd felt at his laugh. "You
didn't push me into it. The place was the way it was because I just didn't know what to do with it and I didn't

want my family doing it by fluttering around and being overly concerned about me. You didn't handle it that way and I appreciate that you *do* know what to do with the whole decorating thing. That's sort of what's going on here, isn't it? We're each finding our way through new territory. I'm helping you out where I can, and you helped me out where you could."

He was just so much less flummoxed than she was.

But he was right, they both *were* finding their way through new territory and it did help not to be alone in it.

They were finding their way through new territory and maybe through a little of the old since that warmth lingered in her and she was having a whole lot of trouble keeping her eyes from meandering to the knee that was directly in front of her and up his thick thigh to jeans-encased anatomy that she certainly shouldn't even peek at let alone be thinking about...

"But so far we're doing okay," he went on, pulling her back to her senses. "Immy seems all right, so I don't think we've done any harm. And my house looks better so this is bound to help get my family off my back about it."

"That's good, I guess. And, no, I don't think there's been any harm done to Immy," Kyla agreed.

"When it comes to the business stuff," he said then, "we'll talk through it when you feel up to it, or a little at a time along the way, and, like I said from the start, I'm here for you for that, too—"

"You said something about your family being left in a situation not too different from this," she said, recalling a comment he'd made early on. "Was that when you were a kid and your parents and aunt and uncle and

GiGi's husband—your grandfather—were killed in the plane crash you told me about years ago?"

"It was. I was eight and my brothers, and Jani and I, and all of our cousins moved in with GiGi. H.J. had to come out of retirement because there was nobody left to run Camden Incorporated. He was eighty-eight."

"He went back to work at eighty-eight?"

"He was tough as nails right to the end. But he knew he wasn't likely to be around to run things until we'd all grown up and were ready to take over the business. So he handpicked people he knew he could trust to keep things going after he was gone and until we could step in. I can help you do that for Immy and the travel centers, if you decide to keep them."

"That seems risky…"

"Not if you can trust the people you pick. And I'll help you find those people. You'd still have to become the CEO or the chairman of the board so you'll be able to keep an eye on things and have final say on major decisions—that's what GiGi did after H.J. was gone. But any decision you might need to make you can run by me, or someone in my family or someone knowledgeable in Camden Incorporated who can give you recommendations, too. Who can point out what might not be sound. I'm just saying that it isn't as if you have to personally do everything yourself. The business can continue and thrive and even grow with the right people in place and you just loosely holding the reins, not letting it take over your life."

"And you know the right people?"

"I don't. But I'm related to nine other people who do. And in case you missed it, Camden's is a big organization," he said with a hint of that smile again. "We can dip into our own pool of managers and directors and financial advisors, not to mention the people in Camden's trucking division who will know about that business specifically. I'm sure we can find more than enough applicants whose experience with us vouches for their trustworthiness, who know what you need them to know and who'd be willing to move into a new arena."

"So you don't think I should consider selling?"

"I think we should have some of our financial people take a look at projections and give us an opinion. Then, ultimately, it's up to you. But at least you'll have something to base your decision on. And if you do sell, I'll make sure you get all the help you need managing the money, investing, keeping it growing and safe. One way or another, what I'm saying is that you aren't in this by yourself. I'm here to help."

He'd said that before and she'd merely resented him all the more for the tardiness of his support. She didn't feel that way now. Now there was some comfort in hearing the words.

But just *some* because the only real comfort for Kyla—ever—was in knowing that she could handle anything she needed to handle on her own. Relying on anyone else had always been a disaster for her. In fact, Beau was living, breathing proof of what happened the last time in her life she'd allowed herself to do that— when she'd thought she could rely on him and when she *had* relied on her father to deal with the pregnancy situation.

But in this there wasn't anything else she knew to do.

She had to accept what Beau was offering.

But, as with Beau's assistance with Immy now, she swore to herself that she would only accept his help with the business and financial aspects for the time being. As soon as she knew enough to make the decision about Immy's inheritance and had found those trustworthy people he was so certain would be available to her, she would employ them, watch them like a hawk and take over.

It was the only way she could rest.

And then Beau could go on with his everything-by-the-book, regimented life, and she would move back to her own life—one that might not look exactly the way it had before but certainly wouldn't look like his did.

"When it comes to your job," he went on to say, interrupting her thoughts, "your cousin and her husband knew if something happened to them they were leaving you with a full plate, that you might not be able to keep teaching. That's why they also left you an annual income and the lump sum you'll inherit when Immy turns twenty-one, so you don't have to worry about re-entering the job market if you don't want to. I'm not sure you heard all of that when the lawyer said it."

She'd heard it only vaguely in the midst of feeling as if she needed to duck for cover from everything that seemed to be coming at her like fastballs from a pitching machine.

"It's all overwhelming right now, but like I said before, we'll just take it one step at a time," he added.

One step at a time until she could stand on her own two feet with everything, then she was out the door, she vowed to herself.

But she didn't say it. She merely took a deep breath, exhaled and said, "Okay."

"Feel better?"

"Some" was all she could concede to.

"It's been a long day. Why don't you get some rest? The more you rest the stronger you'll be, and that will help you feel like you can handle all this."

Back where today had begun—with him telling her what to do.

But she knew what he was saying was true, so she stood up from the chair. "When you're right, you're right."

He got off his perch on the desk and they both left the den and headed for the stairs in the entry.

"What about you? Are you turning in early tonight?" she asked along the way, knowing she'd be surprised if he said he was. She was beginning to wonder if he ever slept.

She'd spent two nights here and although she'd gone upstairs before him and been weary both nights, she hadn't found it easy to fall asleep. Thoughts of him—of how near he was, wondering about him, remembering something small or silly either from the past or from the time they'd spent together since then—had made her mind whirl and given her insomnia. But despite being awake late both nights, she hadn't heard him come upstairs to go to bed himself. And he was getting up with Immy for her middle-of-the-night feeding, and then again first thing in the morning, too, long before Kyla went downstairs.

So there was no surprise in his answer. "Me, turn in early? I don't think so. I'll stay down here for a while. I'm not doing too well with sleep since I've been home."

Kyla stopped at the foot of the steps and looked up at him. She constantly catalogued each small detail of his appearance, but now she wondered if, in the process of that, she was missing something else about him—the way she'd overlooked that he was in a pretty big transition of his own.

His family was hovering around him, worrying about him, trying to help.

He was impatient with them.

He was trying to figure out where he fit in.

Those were all things he'd mentioned in passing. But now it occurred to her that he might be going through more than he was revealing.

"Are you okay?" she asked.

He smiled again—a soft, thoughtful smile that once more raised her temperature. "As in, am I carrying around secret physical or emotional tolls of war?"

She nodded.

"I'm not. I'm fine. Fortunately. But I *am* a little off-kilter. I'm having some adjustment issues. And keeping a different pace than I've been used to is getting to me some—it just never seems like I've done enough to wind down to sleeping much."

"You don't *look* tired," she observed.

"Good," he said with a hint of rare vanity, his smile stretching into a grin.

And she was inexplicably pleased that she was seeing so much more of that grin today for some reason. It made his striking blue eyes light up and gain a sexy glint.

Or maybe that was from something else.

She *had* caught him ogling her earlier.

And now he was looking intently at her face, too. Into her eyes…

Then he did something she'd been trying to avoid.

He touched her.

Innocently enough—he just reached out one of those big hands and clasped her shoulder in a bolstering grasp.

But it did exactly what Kyla had been afraid it would—it set off tiny shards of something glittery all through her.

And while she was trying to stop that, his voice got

deeper, sexier, too, and he said, "Everything really will be okay. I will *not* let you down."

Then he leaned over and kissed the top of her head.

Kyla froze and silently shouted to herself that it was nothing!

And yet it made her heart beat hard and fast—exactly the way it had when he'd touched her for the first time when she was sixteen, when he'd kissed her.

But he'd kissed her for real, then, she was quick to remind herself.

This was nothing. *Nothing!*

This was something he could have done to his sister or one of his cousins or his grandmother or any platonic friend, and it wouldn't have made any of them feel what she was feeling.

So she needed to stop feeling it, she told herself firmly.

But his lips were still pressed to her head and his hand was still on her shoulder and her pulse was still racing.

And even though she didn't want to, she was instantly pondering the possibility that he might kiss her a second time...

On the mouth...

And wishing he would...

Then all in one movement he was gone—he straightened up and took his hand from her shoulder.

Her response didn't stop that quickly. Or at all. But she tried not to let it show and merely nodded her acceptance of his comfort and support as if his touch, his kiss, hadn't meant anything *but* that.

Then she said good-night and went up the stairs.

But try though she might, she couldn't keep her traitorous mind from wondering if any of it *had* meant anything.

And fighting to stomp out the ridiculous and unwanted hope niggling at her from deep inside that it might have…

Chapter Five

Friends and employees of Eddie and Rachel were responsible for the memorial service held on Saturday, and Kyla was grateful to have Beau there with her.

She didn't know anyone who attended except Eddie's secretary and David Cannary. But while no one else knew her, either, the fact that she had Immy and they were the only two family members there meant she was the recipient of all condolences.

Kyla hadn't expected that and wasn't prepared for it. As a result, it was one more thing that felt like too much coming at her. But Beau never left her side, offering her support in that tall, sentry-like way of his that exuded strength and somehow helped her get through it.

"Ready to go home and crash?" Beau guessed when it was finally over. They were back in his SUV with Immy sound asleep in her car seat.

But actually Kyla *wasn't* ready to go home and crash,

she realized. Healthwise she'd been right in assuming that each day she would feel better and stronger. Her aches and pains were dwindling, and even her bruises were fading into something less angry looking. Her wrist and hand were no less weak or sore if she tried to use them, but other than that, she was well on the mend.

And now that the memorial service was behind her, being in the fresh summer air, away from the confinement of a hospital, a motel room or even Beau's beautiful house, felt good.

So she told him that. "You said everything about Denver seems different and you don't remember how to get places anymore—want to just drive around until it all gets familiar again?" she suggested.

"We could. Or if you're up to it and don't want to go home…how do you feel about rugby?"

"Rugby?" she repeated. "I don't have any feelings about it because other than knowing that it's a sport of some kind, I couldn't even tell you what kind of game it is. You like rugby? Did that happen in college or something? Did you play?"

"I played football for USNA. But today is the International Defense Sevens Rugby Tournament at Buckley Air Force Base and navy is playing army—"

"That's a big deal?" she said, interpreting his tone.

"Oh yeah! We wouldn't have to stay long, but I'd like to see some of it."

"With Immy?" Kyla said skeptically.

"She just went to sleep, so she could be out for a couple of hours. We'll keep her shaded, and we have diapers and an emergency bottle if we need them. And we can always leave if she gets unhappy or you get tired or start to wilt or just hate it—"

"Do they have hot dogs?" That was the only redeeming quality she'd ever found in sporting events.

He laughed. "I don't know, but I'd say it's likely. And I'll buy you all you want."

"Rugby…" she said, making the single word a goad. "In a suit and tie?"

The suit and tie she'd had to help him choose because he was too used to having an assigned uniform for every occasion. The black suit he looked fantastic in.

"Rugby," he confirmed. "In a shirt and pants." He'd removed the suit coat before getting behind the wheel and now he tugged on the knot of his gray tie to unfasten it, pulling the tie free of his collar and disposing of it in the console between them before he loosened his top collar button.

All with Kyla watching and enjoying the sight far more than she wanted to.

"At least you're not in a dress," he added with a nod at the black slacks and white blouse she'd worn.

Kyla was *not* a sports person. But he seemed almost excited by the prospect—something she hadn't seen in him since they'd reconnected—so she couldn't say no. "Okay. But if there aren't hot dogs…" she pretended to threaten.

"I'll ask at the gate—no hot dogs, no rugby," he promised as he started the engine.

But Kyla knew that whatever the hot dog answer was at the gate, she was about to attend a rugby game.

Because while she had no interest in it, she *was* curious to see if the new Beau Camden might be able to let himself go—even a little—cheering on his team.

It was almost nine o'clock that night when Kyla headed downstairs after her second shower of the day.

Sitting in a stadium in the August heat had left her hot and sticky, and she'd come home with the goal of a shower to cool off.

It was something Beau said he also wanted, but after sleeping through the entire rugby match, Immy had woken up cranky and out of sorts, putting a delay on everything while they both tried to calm her down.

Fearing the baby had gotten too hot—in spite of keeping her shaded—they'd given her a lukewarm bath. But that had only made her madder, and she'd really been unappeasable after that.

Kyla had finally told Beau to go ahead and take his shower while she tried all the various choices of movement of the bouncy seat—none of which had worked—and then he'd taken over so she could shower.

Kyla had hurried, but her shower had still taken longer than his. She'd washed her hair and had to dry it and use the curling iron again. Plus, although the sun had left her with plenty of color in her cheeks, she'd reapplied a bit of eyeliner and mascara—because although she insisted to herself that she shouldn't care how she looked to Beau, she did care and no amount of calling herself vain changed it.

She'd opted for a pair of khaki capri pants and a cap-sleeved green boatneck T-shirt, but she skipped shoes, relishing the feel of cool flooring under her bare feet.

The nursery door was still open when she left the guest room and passed by it, so she knew Beau hadn't put the baby to bed yet. But as she went down the stairs she couldn't hear Immy's crying, either, and wondered if he'd finally persuaded the two-month-old to take the bottle she'd been refusing.

Fingers crossed, Kyla nearly tiptoed across the entryway for fear of making a sound that might startle Immy and begin the crying again.

At least I'm not alone with it this time, she thought as she went in search of Beau and the baby, recalling her miserable night at the truck-stop motel.

Beau didn't have the baby in the kitchen, so Kyla padded through there to get to the family room connected to it, and that was where she found them.

But Beau wasn't feeding Immy.

He was watching a muted television and didn't see Kyla, and for a moment she stood there taking in the sight of him. And Immy.

After his shower he'd returned wearing a pair of worn-thin jeans and a white crew-neck T-shirt, his short hair slightly damp and his face cleanly shaven. Now he was stretched out on the sofa with the pajama-clad baby lying on his chest, sound asleep on her tummy, her tiny body molded to him, peacefully riding up and down with each of his breaths as he rubbed her back with a hand that was nearly as big as she was.

It had been nice to see Beau spontaneously jumping to his feet to cheer on the navy rugby team that afternoon, to see him elatedly high-fiving the stranger sitting on the other side of him in the stands, so involved in the match that he let down what little hair he had. But seeing him lying there with Immy did something more than merely please Kyla the way seeing him at the game had.

For just a split second the past and the present somehow merged in her mind, making it seem as if Immy was the baby that was lost so long ago, as if Beau was the Beau she used to know—and love—lying there with their own baby. As if she was looking into the life she'd fantasized them having together when she'd realized she was pregnant. When she'd written that letter to him.

And it was a sight that got to her. Touched her. Drew her in.

It was a scene she had to fight not to want to be a part of. Fight to keep herself from crawling onto that couch beside him to curl up against him, too, to wrap her arm around him and that baby at the same time...

But no sooner did that thought pass through her mind than she shoved it away.

This was now, not then! she reminded herself in no uncertain terms.

This was Immy, not their lost baby!

And everything had changed. They had changed.

What they'd had that summer was just a fleeting teenage romance, and she needed not to lose sight of that. They weren't teenagers anymore. The feelings from that summer were long, long gone.

Now, no matter how attractive he was, he was wound too tightly for her. He was too domineering. The strength and steadfastness she'd admired in him as a boy might as well have been on steroids in the grown-up Beau. He was too unwavering. He needed troops to command and she wasn't enlisting.

In all of her growing up years, her parents hadn't told her what to do as much as he had this week, and she didn't take well to it. She couldn't imagine a whole life of his schedules and insistent suggestions and trying to whip her into military shape. She couldn't imagine living with Mr. Rules-And-Regulations and having to negotiate for knickknacks forever.

And she'd drive him crazy, too, she told herself. Sometimes she had projects for school or report cards or paperwork sitting out for days. The clutter and mess didn't bother her, but she had only to look around his shipshape house to know he wouldn't be able to stand it.

Plus she had Immy to think of now. And while Kyla might not have a clear vision of how to raise her, she did know that she didn't want any part of it to look like marine boot camp—which she had no doubt was what any kids raised by Beau were in for.

Beau was Mr. Hospital Corners. Mr. Efficiency. Mr. By-The-Book. And she wanted not one iota of that for herself, or for Immy, either.

What he needed, Kyla insisted to herself, was one of the military-looking women she'd seen at the rugby match. Several of them had clearly cast him glances and checked his ring finger. A few of them had gone on stealing glimpses of him even after realizing he was with her.

And while she'd wanted to scratch their eyes out, now she told herself that a woman like that was what Beau needed—Mrs. Hospital Corners, Mrs. Efficiency, Mrs. By-The-Book. Someone who thrived on regimentation and scheduling and order as much as he did. It would be a match made in heaven.

But her? She was exactly wrong for him.

And he was exactly wrong for her.

But to see him like that…

With a baby…

To think that there once was a baby of their own—hers and his…

She couldn't help having pangs.

But they were pangs she worked to squelch the same way she resisted noticing his biceps or his pecs or his massive thighs or his great derriere or how his eyes got that soft, sweet look in them sometimes when Immy nuzzled into his amazing chest…

No! They weren't right for each other and that was all there was to it, she told herself.

"Oh. Hey."

Beau noticed her just then and his whispered greeting broke into her thoughts, jolting her out of them.

"Hey," she whispered back, finally moving from the doorway into the family room.

Of course she wouldn't let herself crawl onto the sofa with him, but she couldn't keep from going to stand beside the couch to glance down at the sleeping child. She couldn't keep from putting a hand on Immy's tiny rump and connecting herself just a little to the two of them lying there.

"I got her to take most of her bottle," Beau whispered.

"And probably already rinsed it and put it in the dishwasher," Kyla muttered to herself in a futile effort to keep in mind that they just weren't right for each other.

Despite how low her voice was he heard it and said, "No, it's over there on the mantel. I was hoping to get her to take more of it. I didn't, though. And she was still fussy and I didn't know whether to put her in her bed like that or not. Somehow we ended up like this and I don't know why, but it was the magic bullet."

Kyla didn't find that difficult to believe, not when she was also fighting some envy of Immy's position along with everything else.

"I guess I should probably just try to put her to bed now and hope she stays asleep, huh?" he said then.

"Unless you want to stay that way from now until the middle-of-the-night feeding." Because Kyla couldn't imagine that the baby would alter things if she didn't have to—certainly in that position Kyla wouldn't.

"Okay, here goes," Beau said.

Kyla took her own hand away as he slid the hand that was on the infant's back up enough to brace her head and neck, too, and replaced Kyla's hand with his other one to hold Immy tightly to him as he got up from the sofa.

"How'd we do?" he asked, craning his head in an attempt to see Immy's face.

"Still asleep," Kyla answered. "I'll go up with you and make sure the bed is clear so you can just put her down."

Beau nodded at that and Kyla led the way, taking a receiving blanket out of the crib once they'd reached it.

"Should she be wrapped up?" she asked Beau as he came up to the crib alongside her.

He shrugged. "Let's not rock the boat. I'll put her down and you cover her with the blanket. If she wakes up I'll try the burrito-wrap thing."

Kyla waited for him to carefully put Immy in the crib. Then she covered her with the lightweight blanket and—since Immy had remained asleep through the transfer—they left the nursery.

They both breathed a sigh of relief when they reached the hallway and no sounds of crying followed them.

"Okay. Dinner," Beau said, still whispering even though they were headed back down the stairs. They'd both had hot dogs at the stadium, but that had been midafternoon. "Want the shepherd's pie or shall we order something in?"

When they'd gotten home they'd found a note on the counter from his sister Jani—who apparently had a key and had been there while they were out. The note said that she'd brought them the pie, a salad and some rolls for dinner—all in the refrigerator—and some ice cream in the freezer for dessert.

"I'm fine with what Jani brought," Kyla said. "I don't cook much, so it's a treat to have what your family makes."

"Definitely better than MREs."

"MREs?"

"Meals Ready to Eat—the military's version of a sack lunch in combat. Not what you eat if you have any other choice. I've had more than my fair share, so I'm happy to have the home-cooked stuff, too—that part of civilian life doesn't take any adjusting to."

In the kitchen once again they surveyed what Jani had left and slipped into the rhythm they'd developed for meal preparation—Beau doing anything that required two hands and Kyla doing whatever could be done with one.

They ended up sitting across from each other in the breakfast nook with two plates of meat-and-vegetable-laden shepherd's pie, a green salad dressed with what Beau said was Jani's special blend of oil, vinegar and herbs, and buttered bread.

"I thought the memorial service was nice today," Beau said as they started to eat. "Your cousin and her husband had a lot of friends."

"I didn't realize how many. But it *was* nice. There were even some funny parts—I didn't know they met by Rachel crashing into Eddie's car."

"A new Lamborghini five minutes off the dealer's lot—it *must* have been love at first sight for him to be able to forgive her for that."

"That's what Rachel always did say. Now I know why."

"From what I remember of the memorial service for my family after the plane crash there weren't any upbeat stories. It was all pretty serious. But I was only a little kid, so I might have missed something."

"Everybody kept saying how sad it was that Immy would never know Eddie or Rachel, but at least she isn't old enough to go through the kind of grief you must have," Kyla observed. During their summer together they'd talked very little about anything but the present, so there was much she didn't know about him. Before that and after it, too.

"She'll wonder about them and be glad to have those pictures everyone brought," Beau said with the voice of experience. "Whoever thought to suggest that to everyone must have realized it—and that whatever your cousin and her husband had themselves went with the fire. But, yeah, otherwise I'd say never knowing them might be easier for Immy. After the plane crash even the youngest of us still remembered our parents and our lives at home, and we all went through some stuff early on that Immy won't have to."

"Your grandmother had her hands full—ten grieving kids…"

"She did. And H.J. and Margaret and Louie, too."

Kyla knew Margaret and Louie were the housekeeper and groundskeeper-maintenance man hired decades ago by the Camdens. They had ended up helping to raise the Camden grandchildren and were now considered members of the family. Kyla had met Margaret when she stopped by the house.

"We'd spent plenty of time at GiGi's, so we were at home there," Beau went on, "but it still wasn't where we'd all *lived*. And we'd all lost our parents. Death is kind of a weird concept when you're a kid—or at least it was for me. I didn't tell anybody, but it took a long time for me to stop thinking that my mom and dad weren't still just going to walk in the door like they did after a vacation. It took me a long time to stop thinking that everything would go back to the way it was. And I think I was eleven or twelve before I stopped thinking here and there that I'd heard one of their voices or that I'd seen one of them in a crowd."

And she could tell that he hadn't told anyone. He'd just carried it around with him. The way he seemed to do with whatever he was going through now, transitioning from the military to civilian life.

"I think it's probably better that Immy won't have that kind of grief to deal with," Kyla said. "You seemed okay by that summer we met, though. Happy."

"I was," he agreed. "Especially since I knew I was getting into Annapolis."

"Was it everything you wanted it to be?"

"It was," he admitted as if he wasn't sure he should.

"Was it all military this and military that or were there wild parties and fooling around like at regular college?"

He laughed. "That's what yours was like?"

"I couldn't afford to live on campus—I went to UCLA, but I had to commute, so it was mostly just going back and forth for classes."

"Well, mine was mostly military this and military that," he answered her question. "It was a combination of education and preparation for the service. Socializing happens, but there's really not much time for it and too much of it is a distraction. Standards are high and hard to meet—I pretty much stuck to what I was there for."

"But you met a lot of people..." she said, wondering about the female people he might have met.

"Sure," he said, giving her nothing with that answer.

So she went a little further and said, "Girls?"

"A few—but there are a lot more men than women at USNA and in the Marines."

"Anyone special?"

"No," he said without having to think about it— something that pleased her. Until he said, "I did get pressured into taking my roommate's sister to the Ring Dance because that's a big deal and my friends wouldn't let me go stag."

"The Ring Dance? What's that? You put on some kind of headgear and dance rings around tanks?"

He laughed. "Uh…no. The Ring Dance is all pomp and circumstance and ceremony—before it gets to the dancing and cutting loose. It's more formal than a prom—even fancier gowns for the women, dress whites for midshipmen—"

"Midshipmen?"

"That's what students are called—fourth class midshipmen are freshman, third class are sophomores, second class are juniors, first class is senior year. The Ring Dance is when second class midshipmen formally receive their class rings—an original design for every year since 1869. At the Ring Dance chaplains mix water from the seven seas, the rings are dipped in it and then presented as the symbol that you're wedded to the navy. There aren't any tanks involved."

"And you went with your roommate's sister?"

"Yeah. I'd hung out with her sometimes when she came to visit Trey—"

"Hung out, not dated?"

"No, just hung out. She was dying to go to the dance, though—it's a huge social event and Trey's family lived in Maryland, so Tracy knew all about it. Trey said it would be like a dream come true for her—"

"Just to go to the dance…not to go with you…" Kyla

said, her tone laced with doubt because she couldn't imagine that he wouldn't have been the real appeal.

Beau laughed again. "Just to go to the dance. Trey came from a long line of marines and going to the Ring Dance was as close to anything military that Tracy wanted to get."

"So you didn't date her after the dance, either?"

"I didn't."

"And then you went into the Marines," Kyla said. "Was there much opportunity for dating then?"

He laughed once more but stared pointedly at her as he finished a mouthful of meat and gravy. Then he said, "We're doing a dating history here? Is that something you really want to hear about?"

Kyla shrugged. As much as she didn't want to hear about him being with anyone else, she was still too curious not to punish herself with the information. "It's just that it occurred to me that—in the whole spectrum of things—we weren't together for long. And we were kids. You've lived a lot since then and for all I know..." She almost said *for all I know you met the love of your life*, but she didn't want to know if that was true, so instead she said, "...you could have been married and divorced. Two or three times."

"Along with three deployments to the Middle East? That might have set some kind of record. But no, I've never been married or divorced."

"But I'm not the last girl you were with." The words came out before she'd thought about them and after hearing them, she wished she hadn't said them.

But she had and she got an answer.

"No, you're not the last girl I was with," he said with a sort of kindness in his voice as if to cushion the blow.

"I don't suppose I was your one and only, either, but I'm not sure I want to know that."

Kyla didn't know why she was so driven to pursue a subject that was painful for her, but she was. So she said, "Was there something so serious that you don't want to talk about it? Did you fall head over heels for a lady marine and lose her?"

"I lost people in combat who were important to me, but not romantically. There are some rules about who an officer can…get involved with, and I had an across-the-board don't-mix-business-and-pleasure policy. I was never with a woman in the service. Well, when I was in the service, anyway…"

It was frustrating that he still wasn't giving her any actual information and that spurred her to challenge him. "So I *was* your one and only?"

His smile was sheepish. And indulgent. "In some ways," he said under his breath before he finally gave her what she was trolling for. "There was a British war correspondent for a while—we met on base and I spent leaves and liberties with her when we could arrange it—once in London, she showed me around."

That sounded sophisticated and cosmopolitan to Kyla, causing not only a rush of jealousy but also a low feeling of being terribly pedestrian and unworldly.

But things got better when Beau said, "Her name was Mary and we both knew that we were just passing time together. I was hardly in a situation to build a relationship and she was all about her career and following whatever story was juiciest. I was stationed in Helmand, in Afghanistan, at Camp Dwyer then and that was a hot spot, so she came through there pretty often. But eventually I went out into the field and when I came back to base—she just wasn't there anymore.

She hadn't even left me a note saying goodbye. I had to ask around to find out where she'd gone and I never heard from her again."

"It doesn't sound like that bothered you too much," Kyla said, wondering if he was just hiding it behind that marine stoicism.

But he merely shook his head. "It was a nice diversion when I had some downtime, but that was all. It wasn't going anywhere long-term."

"Did anything?"

He shook his head. "Wedded to the navy, remember? There was a nurse I spent some time with after taking shrapnel in the shoulder—I was sidelined a few months to have surgery to repair the damage. She was good company—a little aid and comfort to recover. But I had a job to do over there and that was where my energies went."

"What about since you've been back?"

"Oh, well, yeah. I have been married and divorced two or three times since then…"

Kyla kicked him under the table for his sarcasm.

He grinned at her and she saw a glimmer of the mischievous side of him that she recognized from long ago.

And liked. A lot. Still.

"In the two months since I've been home I've had one date," he answered her genuinely, then. "One blind date that my grandmother forced me to go on with the daughter of someone she knows at the country club. The date ended at the veterans' hospital."

"That's kind of a weird place to go for a good-night kiss," Kyla said.

But this time his smile was more solemn. "Lily had just left the army—the only date I've ever had with a woman in the service—so my grandmother thought we'd have that in common. But when I went to pick Lily up at her parents' house, she was wearing cammies."

"Camisoles?"

"Camouflage," he corrected. "For a nice dinner out. Her mother was trying to get her to change, but there was no getting through to her and the longer things went on about her clothes, the more I started to see that she was in trouble. She was having problems even remembering that she'd been discharged, that she was back in the States, back in civilian life. She was pretty clearly in crisis. We didn't end up going out. Instead I talked her into checking herself into the hospital to get some help and when she agreed, that's where I took her."

That *was* serious, just not the kind of serious Kyla had been expecting.

"As much as I didn't want to go on the date, it was good that GiGi set it up before Lily went too much further off the deep end. That can be a problem bigger than just adjusting."

"But that's honestly all you're going through— adjusting? Because you might not be wearing camouflage, but you *do* always wear something that has some kind of mention of the military on it." She nodded at the insignia on the pocket of his shirt.

He glanced down at it and breathed a small chuckle. "Huh…I didn't even realize that," he said. "But that's really only a sign that I haven't done a lot of clothes shopping since I've been back. I have those couple of suits I showed you this morning for whenever I do something with business—or to go to things like today—and a few clothes to wear to Sunday dinner at GiGi's because she doesn't allow jeans at those, but otherwise…"

He shrugged just one of those broad shoulders and it

occurred to Kyla that wounded or not, they were both still something to see.

"Otherwise I just have stuff I've had for years and years, mostly what I bought in college or on base. There isn't any other deeper meaning to it."

"Are you sorry you're out?" she probed anyway, unsure if he was being completely truthful.

"There's a part of me that is," he seemed to confide. "You're pretty much the only blip in a lifetime of aiming for the military. Everything else I did from the time I was a little kid was to get me there. It's been my life, and now it's over and done with."

Kyla tried not to stall on the thought that she'd been a blip in his goals somehow because it really was him she wanted to hear about tonight.

"But your *life* isn't over or done with," she felt compelled to say.

"No, it isn't," he agreed without any hesitation or sign that he thought that, and she was glad to hear it because it helped dispel some alarm that he might be having more dire issues than she'd assumed. "Just one chapter is."

"Seems like more than one chapter—maybe the first volume in the books of your life."

He smiled at her. "There are going to be *volumes*?"

She shrugged again, allowing for the possibility. "Why did you leave the Marines—since it doesn't really sound like you wanted to?" she asked.

"Things were happening here that I thought it was important for me to help with. I was on the short list for a promotion—"

"To?"

"Major. But there aren't that many of those spots

to go around. I didn't think I should accept it and then leave."

What things were happening here?

That was what Kyla wanted to ask, but he'd said it so ambiguously that she had the sense he didn't want to expound on it. She decided not to pry. Instead she asked, "If things weren't happening here would you have stayed in longer?"

"Probably. It's in my blood."

"So being out is going against your nature?"

"I hope not. I hope it just feels that way for now and that I'll get used to the slower pace. To the lack of discipline. To the hours—maybe someday I'll actually be able to sleep past zero-five-thirty. And think of it as five thirty a.m. I hope I can stop craving being busier, having more work to do. That I won't miss the adrenaline rush of the physical situations. That I'll feel more in touch with everything out here—my family, whatever job I end up doing for Camden Incorporated, everything."

"But that *is* how you feel now?" she said.

"Like a fish out of water—that's how I feel," he summed up. "But it's been better the last few days. Maybe I'm mellowing…" he added, looking steadily at her as if she had something to do with that.

But Kyla could only stare back at him in disbelief. "This is you mellow? The schedules and the perfection and the nothing ever out of place for more than a minute? And remember I saw your closet this morning when you asked me to help you pick out a suit—your shoes are all lined up, toes in, heels out, the same amount of space between each pair, the same as the space between every hanger. You move without making a sound, you hear things I don't think even dogs can hear, you always seem on the alert. Sometimes I'm not even sure you blink and I wonder if they took you, replaced your parts with robot parts and have now just sent you out among us…"

"Wow. I didn't know it was that bad," he said with another laugh.

"It's not *bad*." She refuted the idea quickly. She hadn't meant to offend or criticize him. "But it isn't *mellow*, either."

"I guess I just *feel* more mellow. But I can guarantee one thing—none of my parts have been replaced."

Ah, he still had it in him to put a little innuendo in that—maybe there was hope for him yet.

"I know what you're saying, though," he said then. "I'm still more marine than civilian. I don't know if that will ever change."

And to prove it, since they'd both been finished eating for perhaps five minutes, he stood to clear the table.

Kyla did, too, though she would have preferred to just sit awhile longer.

"Do you want it to change?" she asked as they took everything to the sink.

"Do I want to become a civilian slacker and turn into everything that's driving me crazy?"

"Well, no. But—"

"I don't know what I want right now," he confided. "Fish out of water, remember? There *are* days when I just want to jump back into the bowl. So right now I'm doing what I've told you to do—I'm taking it one step at a time, not making any big decisions, and just trying to make things work. I love my family—even if I am having some trouble fitting in again—and I'd like to get back to being close to them. And I do feel as though I have an obligation to take a role in the business, not to just profit from it. I was raised by H.J. to know that that was expected of me even if I did serve in the military first. I'm just trying to work it all out—let go of the old path and get on a new one, I guess."

"Have you thought about merging paths rather than leaving one completely behind to get on the other?"

He frowned at her as he handed her a rinsed dish to put in the dishwasher. "I don't think Camden Incorporated wants to go to war."

"No, but what about doing things for veterans *through* Camden's? You could instigate a discount for military personnel and their families. You could initiate programs. For instance, you could offer veterans who want to start businesses what you're offering me—help learning how to handle finances and administration. Camden's could sponsor programs to retrain veterans and help get them back into the work force. Or outreach programs to employ veterans yourself. It seems like there are a lot of things that an organization like yours—with the kind of resources you have—could offer. And who would know better than you what former soldiers and military families need? Like with that Lily person—you saw what she needed and got her help. Maybe helping military and ex-military people in other ways through Camden's could be your role in the family business. Seems like that would still be serving your country and connecting you with the military but also get you back into your life here."

Kyla wondered if she'd gone on for too long and lost him because he didn't say a thing as he handed her the last of the dishes and cleaned the counter and sink. Then he went silently to the freezer and took out the ice cream that was intended for their dessert.

"I just want a little of that," she said when he left the carton on the counter and reached for the bowls.

Still without a word, he didn't take down any bowls at all and instead opened a drawer for two spoons.

Once they'd both taken ample spoonfuls of a velvety chocolate gelato, he seemed to come back to the moment, looking at her again. "You sell yourself short, you know it, Gibson?"

"How so?" she asked.

"There's more behind that pretty face than the cleanup song and how to finger paint. Everything you just said...those are damn good ideas. That's the first thing *anybody* has suggested to me that sounds like something I'd actually like to do."

Oh. That made her feel good...

"I'm glad," she said, as if she wasn't thrilled to know she'd come up with an idea he liked. "Just don't tell me I'll have to become a marine before you'll help me now," she joked to cover her own feelings.

"Yeah, you'd make a lousy marine," he joked in return. "Look at you, barefoot and about to double dip into that ice cream..."

She *was* barefoot and had been about to double dip, but she stopped short and rolled her eyes at him before she took a second clean spoon out of the drawer and used that for an additional bite.

"And you still do that," he said thoughtfully, watching her the whole time.

"What?"

"Hold the spoon up and lick the ice cream off like it's in a cone."

She hadn't thought about that, but she guessed that *was* something she did because there she was doing it.

"You did that all summer in Northbridge," he said,

his voice gone quiet, reflective and an octave deeper. "Every time we got that ice cream we liked from the creamery there—remember?—we'd get a dish and share it. You'd do it every time."

"Is that bad? Another reason I'd make a lousy marine?"

His grin was rakish and secret and raised only one side of that lush mouth of his. "It's not bad, but it would definitely put a strain on the fraternization policies."

He finished his own first spoonful of gelato and took a second clean spoon to have another bite, too, saying as he did, "I've been thinking about Northbridge—what would you say to a trip there on Monday? We could take the plane and fly up, spend the night so it wouldn't be too much for you or for Immy and you'd have a night's rest, then Tuesday we could drive your car back here so you'd have it when it comes time to need it."

"*The plane?* As in, you have your own?"

"The family does. We all have access to it."

To Kyla her car meant her freedom, and a trip to Northbridge was also a solution to several other things she'd been thinking about, so she was in favor of that idea and told him so.

"Actually then I could get my driver's license replaced and I can get more of my belongings—I talked to the principal of my school and put in to have the whole semester off to deal with things here, but Darla needs help making the rent, so she's thinking that the sub in my classroom can be her substitute roommate, too. But I have to clear space for her—"

"We can stay longer than overnight if you want."

"I don't have that much stuff and I'm sure Darla will help me box it, so one day and maybe the next morning to get the driver's license and talk to my bank about sending me replacement ATM and credit cards should be enough. The problem is where to stay while we're there. Our apartment is tiny and I'd hate to have Immy keeping Darla up at night when Darla has to go in to work the next day."

"I thought we'd all stay at the ranch. There's plenty of room—it was built for the lot of us to be there at once and it's big enough that not even Immy's crying will bother Seth or his wife—or you, so you can still sleep through the middle-of-the-night feeding."

"You're sure?"

"Positive," he said. "Seth has been trying to get me up there since I've been home anyway. This will kiss...I mean, this will *kill* two birds with one stone."

Kiss? That was an odd slip of the tongue. But he *was* still watching her eat ice cream. Was that what he was thinking about while he did it?

It certainly put it in her mind all of a sudden.

But Kyla retreated from the thought, reminding herself that they were wrong for each other and deciding that if that was what was on his mind, she should call an end to tonight.

So in a tone that relayed that she was ending the evening, she said, "Okay then—Monday to Northbridge, and tomorrow is your family's Sunday dinner?"

He nodded, apparently willing to skirt over the gaffe, too. "Drinks are at five, dinner is at six, but GiGi wants us to come earlier in the afternoon—she says she wants time with you and Immy since I banned her from coming over here. I think I'm being cast as the big, bad ogre."

"Well, you are kind of big and bad..." Kyla teased him, for some reason finding it impossible to block the mental image of how she'd found him when she'd come downstairs earlier. The appeal of seeing him in that softer pose, feeling once more all she'd felt—pangs and urges and drives...

He closed the space between them.

"Yeah, you have no idea how big and bad I can be," he countered her taunt, doing some mock intimidation before he reached for her empty spoon.

But it wasn't intimidation she felt when he came close. When she looked up into his handsome face and found those blue eyes looking down at her from so nearby, full of something she couldn't quite interpret. Or at least something she was afraid to interpret because it seemed primitive and sensual and much like pure, raw desire...

Then suddenly his mouth was on hers in a kiss that was anything but big or bad or intimidating. A spontaneous kiss that was sweet and gentle and as light as their first kiss when they were kids.

And over just as quickly, before she was even able to respond or compare whether or not he'd improved since then.

But at least it wasn't on the top of my head, she thought before she told herself that there shouldn't be any kissing of any kind, anywhere, going on.

"That's probably not a good idea," she heard that saner, more reasonable, rational part of her say while another part of her was reeling.

"We can't turn back the clock," he added, sounding sane and reasonable and rational himself, even as she looked up into those smoldering blue eyes.

"We can't," she agreed.

Or was she telling him that they couldn't kiss? Because they couldn't!

Except that he did it again anyway—taking her just as much by surprise.

Only this time it wasn't over in an instant. And she did kiss him back. And had time to compare...

And, oh, yeah, he'd learned a thing or two because it was an incredible kiss, one that pressed her head farther back, that swayed a little and drew her in...

Until he stopped it, stood up soldier straight again and put both of their ice cream spoons in the sink beside Kyla as if nothing of consequence had happened.

And while she ordered herself to tell him not to ever kiss her again, to make him promise that he wouldn't, she didn't take that order any better than she'd taken any he'd given her. The best she could muster was to stand away from the countertop and say, "Behave yourself, marine!" in a way that didn't sound at all serious.

But when his response was a very businesslike, "Affirmative," she couldn't help feeling a little let down.

And confused.

Yes, she knew very well that kissing didn't have any part in this agreement between them. But she also knew that Beau was likely to have taken what she'd said to heart, carved it in stone and he *wouldn't* ever kiss her again.

And even though that was the way it should be, she couldn't feel anything good about that possibility.

But she concealed her feelings with a fortifying breath and said, "The memorial service, and rugby, and the heat, and hours of crying baby—that seems like a full enough day. I think I'll say good-night."

Beau nodded. "'Night," he said, as if she'd already been dismissed. Kyla turned tail and left him in the kitchen.

But when she reached the foot of the stairs she hesitated to go up, glancing back at him.

He wasn't standing stick straight anymore. Instead, he had both hands flat to the counter she'd been leaning against, arms out, elbows locked, bracing his weight as he stared down at the marble.

Locked inside of himself. Lost in thought.

But about what? Kyla wondered.

About putting his life on a new course and starting to resolve some of the issues he had?

Or about her?

About those kisses—the one last night and the two just now?

Probably not the kisses, she decided. Even if those kisses were so much on *her* mind that she knew she was going to have trouble falling asleep tonight, too.

Thinking about them.

Especially about that last one.

And the way it had felt to have his mouth on hers again…

New.

And not so new.

Chapter Six

Push-ups. Pull-ups. Crunches. Weights.

Beau wasn't counting the sets or the reps he was doing before dawn on Sunday morning. He was just in his basement gym, pushing himself through the most grueling workout his body would withstand.

Immy wasn't awake yet and he'd had even less sleep than usual, this time because he was so disgusted with himself. And not knowing what else to do with that disgust—or the whole slew of other feelings that seemed to be holding him under siege—he'd come down to the gym to try to work it out of his system.

Discipline. He needed discipline. He was a marine and marines were disciplined. When they knew better than to do something, they didn't do it.

And he knew better than to go around kissing Kyla.

But he had anyway.

Friday night there was that stupid kiss on the forehead that was supposed to look like nothing but comfort and support—but who was he trying to fool? He'd just needed to touch her. To get closer to her. To kiss her. Landing it on her forehead rather than her mouth was as far as discipline had gotten him that night.

And last night?

Last night was even worse—he'd kissed her on the mouth. Twice. And it was still nothing compared to what he'd wanted. But he just kept giving in to the damn weakness he had for her—that was the problem.

And God help him, he had a weakness for her...

She was on his mind every minute and not only because he was taking care of her—he wasn't merely thinking about whether or not she was overdoing it, or when she should rest, or if she seemed to be on the mend and how to help get her there.

No, he was thinking about the way her hair shone like silk.

He was thinking about her dark amber eyes with their streaks of honey gold.

He was thinking about how small and cute her nose was.

He was thinking about how downy her skin looked and aching to brush the side of her beautiful face with the backs of his fingers.

He was thinking about how much he liked the sound of her voice, of her laugh. About the way she looked when she smiled and flashed those damn dimples.

He was thinking about the view he got when she walked out of a room—of that perfect, tight rump.

He was thinking about keeping his eyes from drifting down to her chest. And how much he wanted to get his hands on it.

And yes, he was thinking about her mouth, her lips.

How he hadn't been able to get enough of kissing her that summer. How much he wanted to kiss her now...

As if he were still a hormonal kid who didn't have years of training and conditioning and discipline to teach him how to control himself.

Get a grip! he mentally shouted as he picked up heavier dumbbells to do more biceps curls.

This was no time to get involved in any relationship. He had to find his way in this new chapter—this new *volume*—of his life before he could let anything like that happen.

He wasn't messed up from his time in the service. He honestly wasn't. Lily had been messed up. He had friends who were messed up. He knew what it looked like. What he had problems with was exactly what he'd told Kyla.

Adjusting to things, getting his bearings, figuring out this next part of his life was still something to deal with. Enough to deal with to leave no room in his life for romance or relationships.

Any relationship, let alone one with the extra complications of the past he and Kyla shared.

Because that was part of what had happened last night. What had tripped him up.

He wasn't ever with her without being attracted to her, without wanting to touch her, to smell her hair, to kiss her. To do more than kiss her.

But just when he'd thought he was keeping it all contained she'd taken that spoonful of ice cream...

And he'd flashed back to their summer in Northbridge.

To when they were just those two teenagers, wild about each other.

And he'd been lost all over again.

He'd confused fourteen years ago with now. And

he had no idea what were old feelings and what might be new.

Were things like last night just a retreat from his current problems? A return to that summer, to that first brush with love and awakening and desire and pure, raw sexual energy?

Or was there more to it? Had it come out of the people that they were now? Out of the time they were spending together? The talking? The connecting?

He couldn't deny that he liked spending time with her, talking to her. He was even opening up to her a little in a way he hadn't been able to open up to his family, or to anyone, since he'd gotten back.

But he hadn't lost his grip until he'd flashed back to that summer.

So he couldn't be sure what were memories and flashbacks and what weren't.

And as long as he couldn't be sure, he couldn't run the risk that he was just escaping what he was going through now by replaying something that had felt good a long time ago.

Because if that's what he was doing, down the road he could wake up and realize that he'd been using Kyla—using what they'd had in the past to make him feel safe and comfortable in his world here and now. And he never—*never*—wanted her to ever again think that he saw her as someone to be used.

And as long as he couldn't sort through it and know for sure, he couldn't act on anything.

He *needed* things clear-cut. Black and white. Strong lines of distinction.

Murky waters were dangerous.

And these were murky waters.

Besides, it wasn't as if Kyla had given him any signs of encouragement.

Sure, she was still Kyla—sweet and kind and softhearted, thoughtful and caring and compassionate. With that twist of pluck and sass thrown in.

And, yeah, sometimes he caught her watching him, looking at him with something in her eyes that he wanted to believe was attraction to him, too.

But she was so careful to make sure they never had any physical contact when they handed Immy back and forth. So careful to keep things strictly friendly. There was no flirting. Nothing coy. Nothing that he could take as an invitation.

And she couldn't be thinking the same things about him that he was thinking about her or she wouldn't have stiffened up when he'd touched her Friday night.

She wouldn't have been so wide-eyed when he'd kissed her last night, either.

Although the second time she *had* kissed him back...

But then she'd told him it wasn't a good idea. To behave himself. That was pretty clear.

And he had taken it as a message that she *wasn't* flashing back the way he was. That she wasn't having the same urges and inclinations—old or new.

Which stood to reason, he told himself.

She had to be carrying some scars, some bad feelings about their past—even if he *had* convinced her of his ignorance of what went on back then. She'd still hated him for more than a decade and that had to have left things pretty murky for her, too. Or maybe left them clear-cut in the negative—maybe she was clear on not wanting anything to do with him other than accepting the aid he was giving in her time of need.

She probably just doesn't want you, marine...

Which was why she'd said what she'd said.

So take the hint! he ordered himself.

Besides, he agreed with her. He'd basically given her his word that he wouldn't pursue her any further. So it would be dishonorable for him to kiss her again. Or to do anything else.

He put the dumbbells on their rack and sat down on the end of his weight bench, finally allowing himself the rest every muscle in his body craved.

And as he sat there he realized that he didn't like the conclusion he'd come to.

But, like it or not, he had to accept that things were the way they were.

He had a job to do with Kyla, with Immy. A job he would do, and when he had, that would be it. Over and done with.

That was clear-cut.

So why wasn't there any relief in it?

Maybe because he knew how hard it was going to be to curb his thoughts. And his urges. And get his head straight when it came to Kyla.

How hard it was going to be to walk away from her and Immy, too.

Harder, possibly, than he was finding it to adjust to civilian life.

But that was what he had to do.

That was what he was going to do.

He was going to be marine enough to control himself and to get this job done.

The problem was, while he might be marine enough to suck it up and accept what he didn't like about civilian life, he wasn't absolutely certain that he was marine enough to resist the pull of that particular woman.

* * *

"Ugh! I'm not going to eat for a week!" Kyla moaned Sunday night when she came downstairs after changing clothes.

They'd been home from the Camden family Sunday dinner for about an hour—long enough to give Immy a bottle and put her down for the night.

Then both Kyla and Beau had wanted to get into more comfortable clothes than the casual dress outfits that met GiGi's no-jeans policy, so they'd gone to their separate rooms to change.

Now, wearing a pair of red-and-white polka-dot lounging pants and a white T-shirt, Kyla found Beau in the family room.

He'd gone from slacks and a polo shirt—that he'd pointed out had no military inscriptions or insignias— to a pair of gray sweatpants and another USNA T-shirt. Sitting at one end of the sofa, he was angled from the corner with his right arm stretched across the top of the back cushions and his left across the top of the high side of the soft tufted leather. He looked more relaxed than usual.

Kyla plopped down onto the other side of the couch, her back against the side, her legs stretched out on the cushions so her feet weren't far from his leg, groaning and holding her overly full stomach as she did.

"I've learned to pace myself at Sunday dinner," Beau said with some amusement in his tone as he watched her. "But today it was tough—there's just no beating Margaret's barbecue sauce. It's one of her specialties— her secret sauce. She won't tell any of us the recipe, she says we can have it when she dies."

"Everything else was so good, too," Kyla complained.

He nodded and his grin turned into a more reserved kind of smile. "Yeah, it was."

"Why does it sound like you're talking about more than just the food?"

He shrugged only his left shoulder. "This was the first Sunday dinner since I've been back that I actually..." another shrug "...I don't know, felt comfortable, I guess." Then he seemed to consider that and added, "It was nice having you there. And Immy took some of the pressure off me."

"She was happy being the center of attention," Kyla said, glossing over the fact that he'd liked having her there—which she liked hearing but didn't want him to know.

"Having your suggestion to make to everybody about what I can do in Camden Incorporated helped, too," Beau said then.

"It seemed to go over well."

"It did," he agreed. "Because it's a good idea."

He'd given her credit for it in front of his entire family. That had embarrassed her a little, so she didn't want to talk about it.

"Have you not really liked the Sunday dinners since you've been back?" she asked to change the subject.

"I have," he hedged. "But I've also felt kind of on the spot—*that* I don't like. And there's been that not-fitting-in thing. Today I got to be just one of the gang again—that was great. And it was also great having something to contribute—I wasn't just fielding everybody's pitches about what I might want to or be able to do. I was throwing out some things myself, and that felt really good. How about you? Was it all okay for you?"

"I loved it!" Kyla gushed. "You don't know how many fantasies I had growing up of what a traditional family was like. And there it all was today! Brothers and sisters and cousins, your grandmother and her second-husband-just-since-June—who made me think of a jolly little grandfather—and even Margaret and Louie who might as well be your live-in aunt and uncle. It's just what I hoped having a family was like. I know some of that closeness can feel smothering and has been kind of bothering you, but it was what I always wanted. And they all made it feel like Immy and I were a part of it—at least for today. I loved it!" she repeated.

He nodded again. "Different than what you had."

"*Worlds* different. But it's what I *dreamed* of having." And probably why it had made losing their baby especially difficult, because a small part of her had pictured it as the potential for that family...

An inquisitive frown drew Beau's well-shaped brows together. "So—given that—I would have thought getting married and having a family of your own would have been a priority for you—" He stopped short as something else seemed to occur to him, then said, "Oh...I know you aren't married now, but maybe it's *you* who's been married and divorced two or three times."

Kyla delighted in the expression that idea put on his handsome face because he looked distinctly startled by it. She pretended he'd guessed her secret and, as if it were true, said, "Three times."

But she didn't fool him. His eyes narrowed into slivers of blue. "You haven't been married at all."

Kyla gave up the ghost and laughed. "So you're a human lie detector, too, huh? No, I haven't been married or divorced."

"How come, then—if a big family has always been your dream?"

"I thought you didn't want to know about my dating history," she reminded him.

He seemed to consider that before he said, "Okay, I admit it—I'm curious. But maybe just about the ones who didn't measure up to me…"

"That would have been all of them for a long time," she confessed before she realized she was going to.

"But not for the *whole* time?" he asked with mock offense that she thought might not be completely bogus.

She decided to answer him honestly. "No, not the whole time, because it occurred to me a while ago that I was measuring grown men against…well, against a seventeen-year-old who was as carried away as I was with a summer romance full of bigger-than-life emotions," she admitted. "But we were kids and so what we'd had was kid stuff. And that probably wasn't anything realistic to measure other relationships against. Or to measure other guys against."

"You had grown men who couldn't live up to me as a seventeen-year-old, so you found a way to excuse them?"

"Oh, the ego!" she said, nudging his knee with her foot to chastise him. "Come on," she challenged him. "*You* probably couldn't live up to the romantic seventeen-year-old you were then. I still have a box of things…among them a pair of origami butterflies folded by none other than—"

"Okay, okay," he cut her off with a self-conscious half grin.

She let him off the hook and went on. "So I decided I had to stop comparing things—or guys—to that. And you. And when I finally did, that was when I starting having more than a date or two with anybody."

"How long did it take for you to get there? Till last

month? The month before?" he joked. But again she thought he was not totally pleased to hear she'd gotten over him.

"Shouldn't marines be humble?" she mocked.

He laughed. "All right, let me have it then—the full picture of your *adult* relationships."

"There have only been two guys who were more than just a few dates. There was a musician in California the last year I was there, after my parents died—"

"That was quite a while after us."

Kyla gave him a stern frown from under her brows to silently rebuke him for going back to that.

He got the message and changed tacks. "After everything with your parents, you actually went for a musician?"

"Unlike my parents, Cal was actually successful at it—he writes scores for movies and TV. If I'd met him before, when they were alive, he actually might have been their ticket into the music industry somehow—"

"How did you meet him?"

"In an elevator. Cal had just been to his agent's office and I was picking up all of the demos my parents had given to another, much more sleazy agent in the building. Cal and I were alone in the elevator, he saw the box of demos and thought they were mine, that I was taking them in to someone rather than retrieving them. He used it as an opening to hit on me."

"So maybe *he* was a little sleazy."

"You can think that if you want, but no. He was just making conversation. And he was a nice guy—like I said, if my parents had still been alive I'm sure he would have bent over backward to help them. He even lets music students from UCLA intern with him to learn the business."

"Ah, I get it—he's a saint," Beau said derisively.

Kyla knew from listening to what he'd said about the women in his life that it wasn't easy hearing about replacements, so she ignored his tone.

But she did sort of like the idea that he was jealous.

"No, Cal wasn't a saint, either. He was a pretty regular guy—"

"Who you didn't end up with. Why?"

"He had a big house in Malibu, he really was a success, but... There were still too many similarities to my parents. His feet just weren't on the ground. He had a business manager who paid his bills and a housekeeper who kept the place clean and the refrigerator full, or he would have needed a daughter to do it for him, too. And I just never knew from one minute to the next if he would follow through with promises he made or if he'd forget about everything and everyone to do something that caught his interest or to chase some whim."

"Like your parents."

"Yeah. The last straw was when his mother broke her leg. Cal had decided he needed to hone his skills on the cello, for some reason. He was obsessed with it, day and night. It was me who went to the hospital when her friend called. I sat there alone through the surgery and afterward, and spent time in the hospital with her and found her a rehab center to go to when she was ready to be transferred—"

"He was *still* practicing his cello then—days later?"

"Like my parents, everything fell by the wayside if he was *inspired*. His mom was out of rehab and back at home with a nurse I'd found for her before Cal did more than the occasional phone call or text to her. So there was still that flighty, unreliable...self-absorption...about him. His just seemed more justifiable because he actually *was* making a living off his 'artistic temperament.' But to me—"

"It was flighty and unreliable, and you still had to pick up the slack and be responsible to make up for it."

"Yeah," she admitted. "I don't know…maybe being with him—somebody my parents would have been *thrilled* with—was my tribute to them so soon after they died. Or maybe it was so much like the way things were when I was growing up that it was comforting, somehow, when I'd just lost them. But the longer it went on, the more I knew I didn't want to be with Cal or in California anymore, either. That was when I decided to go back to Northbridge."

Beau nodded sagely, apparently finding that story not as difficult to hear as he'd anticipated. "And back in Northbridge you had another Northbridge romance?" he asked, with a bit of that edge back in his tone, as if he was the only person she was allowed to be romanced by in the small town.

But that *was* where her second serious relationship had been, so Kyla nodded. "I got involved with Northbridge's former city treasurer—Alden Briggs. Divorced. Two kids he *used* to have custody of…"

"*Former* city treasurer and kids he *used* to have custody of? Do the two go hand in hand?"

"Kind of. At least he said that losing them both was my fault," she confessed with a hint of chagrin.

"Why?"

"We met at a back-to-school night the first year I started teaching in Northbridge. His youngest was in second grade, but our paths crossed and things clicked. The next day Alden called and asked me out. And I said yes. I thought he was great—a single dad making sure he did everything right for his kids, conscientious and family oriented—"

"With that family you wanted already started."

"Right. I liked his kids—a boy and a girl—and they liked me. We had as many family outings as dates and everything seemed good." In fact, Alden had seemed like the first person to measure up to Beau.

"Until?"

"Until I realized that Alden wasn't just a *conscientious* parent—he was kind of a tyrant. Those poor kids had to toe the line. Mud on their shoes was a crisis because they were so worried that it would rock the boat with their father. I tried to talk to Alden, to get him to ease up, but he just got mad at me. He said his ex-wife had been lax, too, and that didn't fly with him. He ran a tight ship—his words—and that was the best way, and that's all there was to it."

Kyla wasn't sure if Beau saw the similarities between what she was describing and the way he seemed to like things. He didn't comment on it to agree or disagree that that was how things *should* be.

"Anyway," she continued, "as much like my parents as Cal turned out to be, Alden was too much *not* like them. I just ended up feeling sorry for his kids. Somehow that got back to the kids' mother after I broke it off with him—you know, word travels in a small town. Alden hadn't told me his ex-wife was still battling for custody, and the ex's attorney subpoenaed my testimony at the hearing. I had to say what I'd seen—that the kids were more afraid to mess up than actually well-behaved—and his ex ended up getting custody back."

"Was that bad?"

"I think it was good for the kids—I didn't see or hear anything about their mother that made me think there was something wrong with her, she just hadn't been a match for Alden's iron fist in the courts during the first custody hearing any more than his kids—or I—had been a match for it outside of them."

"She hadn't been a match for him until she had you as ammunition, anyway."

Kyla confirmed that with a shrug. "But the whole thing was ugly and I ended up in the middle of it. Alden was convinced that losing custody made him look bad to voters, so when he lost the next election for treasurer he blamed me for that, too. Like I said, it all got ugly. I was relieved when he moved to Billings."

"And that was all when?"

"About a year ago."

"There hasn't been anybody since then?"

"No. I thought I'd take a little time. Alden sort of shot a hole through what I thought I wanted and I needed to sort that out—"

"How so?"

"Well, Alden seemed great. Exactly what I was look-ing for—the opposite of what I grew up with. A devoted father, family oriented. Organized, settled, reliable. But being with him made me realize that there might be a little of my parents in me—I *don't* want things *too* shipshape—"

"But there has to be a firm foundation. Rules and guidelines, codes of conduct."

Of course he would say that.

"Rules are okay, but I don't think being *bound* to anything, at all costs, is good. Especially when there are kids involved," she argued.

"If you tell fifteen-year-old Immy her curfew is ten o'clock but that she isn't *bound* to that, she'll come home whenever she pleases—you know that, right? Kids test boundaries. And anything you're wishy-washy about is a battle you'll be on the losing end of."

"I'm going to try not to look at raising Immy as waging war," she said. Then, pointing to herself she added, "*Not* a marine—or a city treasurer, either—remember?"

Beau laughed. "You know, I've always heard that comparison made—marines, small-town city treasurers, exactly the same…"

"Maybe not *exactly*," she said, as if the distinction was minimal.

"Because, after all, not even good old *Alden* was me," he said with some exaggerated cockiness, as if that's what she'd meant.

"I don't know…" she said to take him down a peg. "Alden might have been a little too much the *you* you are now."

"And you don't like me now?" he challenged, still cocky.

"Hmm…rugby in sweltering heat yesterday, gluttony today… Those do seem to help, but—"

"Gluttony? You're the one who overate. I told you, I've learned to pace myself."

"Oh, yeah, that's true. The march of the wooden soldier," she said, doing a mock stilted march with her shoulders, stiffly thrusting them back and forth.

Until she realized that Beau's gaze went from her shoulders to the breasts she was thrusting forward, too…

She stopped and his eyes met hers again. One brow rose in challenge as he pivoted in her direction on the couch. "You want me to speed things up?"

She wasn't sure what *things* he was talking about.

Although those two kisses that had left her wanting

more the night before came to mind as he bent forward enough so that she had to lean back to keep her distance.

"Because if you don't like the pace…" he said "…I can do something about that."

She hadn't meant to do anything sexy. Anything tempting or teasing or alluring or inviting. She really hadn't.

But there she was, with his ruggedly sculpted face not far from hers, and even though she planned to tell him she'd just been making a joke, she didn't. Not when suddenly the only thing she could think about was him kissing her again.

In fact, all she could make herself do was raise her chin at him as if she were issuing a challenge of her own.

A challenge that everything in her was screaming for him to accept…

Which he did.

He closed the distance between them as his mouth found hers again. There was nothing sweet or gentle about his kiss tonight. It was a kiss from a man who knew how to kiss and wasn't shy about doing it.

His lips were parted, and after a moment, so were hers. A moment that went on for just so long before mouths drifted open a little more and his tongue came to show techniques he certainly hadn't had at seventeen. Techniques that canceled every thought, every voice in Kyla's head that advised her not to do this, and left her merely kissing him back, meeting every game his tongue initiated and beginning one or two of her own.

Somewhere along the way she slipped down until her head was on the arm of the sofa and her arms went around him—around those broad shoulders her eyes loved to feast on—and she laid her hands to his back, hating the brace on her right that blocked full contact and barely registering any pain in fingers that pressed into him despite it.

She marveled at the feel of improvements to his hard and unyielding body she'd only been able to look at before this.

His arms went underneath her, around her, his mouth opened wider and the kiss deepened as his hands splayed on her back, too.

Big hands she could feel the strength in. Hands that were so much more confident than they'd been the last time he'd touched her.

Hands that coursed over every inch of her back. That rubbed their way down to her hips, then up again in a massage that turned her own muscles to putty and made her yearn for that same thing in front...

But she knew that yearning for anything was dangerous and after letting it go on awhile longer—just because she couldn't make herself stop something so, so good—she took her arms from around him and laid her left palm to his chest.

Granted, it was only feebly at first, because she couldn't resist spending a little time learning the glorious feel of that, too, but then she reminded herself that she'd inadvertently started this and it was up to her to finish it. She used her uninjured hand to push him up.

And up he went, far enough to move to the side slightly and drop his forehead to the couch arm beside hers as he muttered in a deep, raspy voice, "Okay... breaking my own code of conduct already."

"Your own code of conduct?"

"That's what should have kept that from happening after you already told me no last night."

Had she told him no?

He sat up, moved away. "You said it wasn't a good idea," he reminded her.

She had. But that had seemed to her more like an observation than a no...

"You said that I should behave," he added.

And of course he'd taken that as laying down the law.

"I guess I did say that," she agreed.

"So I swore to myself I wouldn't kiss you again."

Kyla was torn between knowing she should tell him to make sure he didn't and just wanting to be kissing him again right that minute.

"It's probably not smart for either of us," she said without a drop of conviction.

"Probably not," he responded without any more of it himself before he said softly, "And I'm trying to care about that, but I'm not having much luck."

She smiled to herself. But she also knew that if she didn't get up, if she didn't move farther away from him, they could easily lapse into making out the way they had as teenagers.

And she wasn't sure where that might go.

So she sat up and swung her feet to the floor, breathing a long, deep sigh.

"I'm not behaving any better than you are, but we should probably try to," she said.

"Probably," he confirmed.

Probably, probably, probably...

But she had the impression that he wasn't taking anything as law tonight because he was agreeing without really committing.

"Northbridge tomorrow," she said then.

"The flight plan has us leaving about an hour and a half after Immy usually gets up in the morning. We use a private hangar, so we don't have to get there too much before that."

Kyla nodded. They'd packed while Immy napped that afternoon. "Darla got a sub for school so she can stay home and help me with the stuff at the apartment if you'll keep Immy with you."

"Sure. But if you need my help I can take care of her at your apartment."

Kyla knew she had to talk to her friend alone. Maybe Darla could give her some perspective on what was going on when it came to Beau, some tools to resist what was urging her right at that moment to just get him to kiss her again.

So she said, "Darla's help will be enough if you'll keep Immy."

"Okay."

Kyla stood to go.

But with one catch of her hand, one tug of her down toward him, he was kissing her again—tongue and all—and she had to fight not to collapse on top of him.

Then he ended the kiss and let go of her.

"Sleep well," he said, his voice raspy again.

"You, too," she answered, knowing it was unlikely for her.

Because she was so confused and baffled and bewildered by what was happening in her when it came to him.

And whatever it all was, it didn't feel like kid stuff.

Which was the scariest thing of all.

Chapter Seven

"It's like hooking up with an old high school boyfriend at a class reunion—you relive some of the past, you get to be nostalgic and feel a little rush, and it might be fun for the reunion weekend. But after that you have to go back to real life. And in real life, you're just not looking for someone as rigid as it sounds like this guy is, Kyla, so where can anything with him go?"

"Nowhere," Kyla answered Darla's question definitively.

They'd been packing since Kyla had arrived in Northbridge that morning. Seth Camden had been waiting at the airport in Billings when the Camden family plane landed and after the drive to the much smaller town, he'd dropped Kyla off at her apartment before taking Beau and Immy on to the ranch.

Kyla hadn't held anything back in telling Darla what was going on with Beau. She'd confessed her attraction to him but also made it clear that she knew she needed to resist that attraction and all the reasons why.

As always the raven-haired, dark-eyed Darla was supportive. And patient, because as the afternoon began to wane and most of Kyla's belongings were loaded into the trunk of her small sedan, Kyla realized that she'd spent the entire time with her friend talking primarily about Beau. Yes, she'd also discussed Immy and the changes she was facing in her life and all she needed to take care of for Immy's future, but still everything had somehow circled back to Beau.

"Right—nothing with him can go anywhere," Darla confirmed as they sat at the kitchen table. "On the other hand," her friend said, "you seem kind of fixated on the guy—"

"Fixated?"

"Fixated, obsessed, infatuated… If I had a nickel for every time you've said his name today I could pay next month's rent. Without any help from a roommate."

"I know," Kyla lamented. "You'd think with all I have going on now with Immy and dealing with her inheritance and becoming a single parent and having my whole life shaken up, that it wouldn't be this guy who's on my mind nonstop."

"You'd think," Darla agreed. "But apparently he is. And since he is…I don't know. Maybe he's unfinished business for you and you have to finish it."

"By cutting it off with him?" Kyla said. "My wrist is getting better, so I'll be able to do everything with Immy soon, and I know I can move into your sister's place in Denver anytime."

Darla had told Kyla just this morning that her sister had decided to move in with her boyfriend and needed someone to take over her Denver apartment for the last three months of the lease.

"But I still need some guidance and tutoring to deal with Immy's inheritance," Kyla continued. "So I'll have to have *something* to do with Beau for a while longer."

"Actually, no, I don't mean you should just cut it off with him. I mean that maybe it's like when you're wishing for peanut butter, you know? You can't stop wishing for it until you get some. Maybe you have to *get some* of this guy before you can close the book on your feelings for him."

Kyla laughed. *"Get some?"*

"Maybe. Like the peanut butter—what do you do every time?"

"I buy a jar, eat a couple of spoonfuls—"

"And then the rest of the jar sits around until I've finished it."

"Because after I've satisfied the craving I don't want any more," Kyla concluded.

"Things never got finished with this guy," Darla went on. "You thought you had reason to hate him and that sort of put an end to it. But now you've found out that you *didn't* have a reason to hate him and maybe that's put it all back to being unfinished. And the fact that he's so hot, well, that just makes it worse. Maybe if you have a few spoonfuls of that peanut butter, you can get past the past and see through his hotness the way you saw through how perfect you thought Alden was. And *then* you can stop fixating and just move on—regardless of what you need him for, for the business and financial stuff."

Kyla laughed again. "That's not advice I expected you to give me."

"I can't even find a way to make you stop talking about him and I know how you are when you need peanut butter, so I don't know what else to tell you. Get some."

They both laughed at that.

Then Kyla said, "But what if he's chocolate and not peanut butter?"

"Oh, then you're in trouble and I guess you better buy marching boots and learn to say *yes sir.*"

Kyla grimaced at that option. "We're really not right for each other," she repeated, as much to herself as to Darla.

"But I don't think you're going to really be able to embrace that until you have those spoonfuls."

Kyla sighed audibly and stood to go. "You were supposed to talk me *off* the ledge," she complained.

Darla shrugged helplessly. "I can't ever talk you out of buying that whole jar of peanut butter, what made you think I'd be able to talk you out of this?"

"Yeah, well, you weren't supposed to talk me *into* it, either."

"I didn't talk you into it. I just presented the *maybes.*"

"*Maybe* you just got me into more trouble."

"Then don't do it. *Maybe* you'll just stop fixating on him any minute now…"

There was a taunt in that because they both knew it was unlikely.

"I was beginning to think you were hiding, marine, scared of what I'm about to show you," Kyla said to Beau when he finally came out of the rear of the ranch's main house at eight thirty that night.

Kyla had arrived from her apartment at five twenty and Beau had walked her to her room at the ranch. She'd showered and changed into clean clothes—a pair of black twill capri pants and a white tank top with braided straps that crossed in back. Then she'd joined Beau, his brother Seth and Seth's very pregnant wife, Lacey, for dinner poolside.

The meal that Seth cooked completely on the barbecue had been accompanied by pleasant conversation with the happily married couple. But afterward Lacey had tired. About the time Beau and Kyla had Immy ready to be put to bed, Seth and Lacey said good-night, too. So Beau had followed the couple inside with Immy in tow and left Kyla waiting for him.

While she waited, Kyla had moved from where they'd all been sitting at a table to a comfortable-looking double-hammock swing chair hanging from a tree at the far side of the tiled pool deck.

And she'd taken with her the old shoe box she'd brought from the apartment and made a mystery out of to Beau.

"You're going to show me something dead? Body parts?" he guessed without any apprehension as he came around the pool.

Kyla shook her head smugly and patted the other side of the swing, inviting him to sit beside her.

He'd showered and changed sometime while she was with Darla and was wearing a pair of jeans and a pale blue mock neck T-shirt. She wasn't sure when or where he'd gotten it, but it looked new and bore no mention of anything military.

It did have long sleeves, though, that he had pushed above his elbows. And even though that blocked the view of the biceps she liked to ogle, the display of forearms she ordinarily overlooked was almost as remarkable.

The color of the shirt also brought out the blue of his eyes and Kyla had been very aware of that all evening.

Accepting her invitation, he sat next to her, making the swing sway. They were separated by only inches and Kyla tried not to think about how much she liked being that near to him.

"Okay, let's have it," he said. "This must be good since you've been trying so hard to build my suspense by shaking it at me and tapping on it every time Seth and Lacey weren't looking.".

She had been taunting him with the box and enjoying the game.

She'd told Lacey ahead of time what was in it, and Seth had accepted her simple explanation of, "It's just some things I took from the apartment today that I thought Beau might like to see later," so no one had pushed for her to open it and she'd placed it under her chair.

"It's proof that once upon a time you had a soft center," she said.

"Did I?" he countered.

She raised an eyebrow at him. "If you didn't, then I'm going back to thinking that you were just some rich boy lying to get what you wanted."

He flinched. "Is that what you thought?"

Kyla answered only with an arch of both eyebrows.

"I wasn't just some rich boy lying to you. You know I wasn't. But if this stuff disappears during the night so it never shows up again to ruin my image I'm telling you ahead of time that it wasn't me who did it."

Kyla smiled smugly again. "Just try to get your hands on it."

The smile that answered that was wicked and she knew her turn of phrase had amused him.

It also occurred to her suddenly that more often than not lately there *was* expression on that handsome face.

The stoicism could come back in a flash, but it wasn't constant anymore. And that was nice.

But she was still determined to have the upper hand, so she ignored the devilish smile and opened the lid on the shoe box that held mementoes of their summer together fourteen years ago.

"I wondered where that went," Beau said the minute the lid was off, immediately spotting a braided leather wristband. Kyla had made it for him and he'd worn it every day that summer.

"I found it in the grass after you left. It must have fallen off that last night." And while she'd been sorry he wouldn't have it to remember her by, she'd also put it around her own wrist and worn it herself to feel closer to him.

Or, at least, she'd worn it until her father had returned from Denver. Then she'd torn it off and thrown it in the trash.

Where it had stayed until the next day when she hadn't been able to stand the thought of losing it—and her memories of Beau—forever. Then she'd retrieved it and jammed it into the shoe box.

"Looks too small now," Beau observed, holding out his left wrist for her to put it on him.

She tried, but he was right, it no longer fit. He really had changed physically from boy to man.

"Would you wear it if it did?" she asked him.

"Mmm…" he mused. "It's not really my style now."

It wasn't. But somehow she was okay with the fact that there were only shadows of the boy left in him, and that made her realize that in some ways she was coming to accept the man he'd grown into. And maybe even like him a little more than she'd expected to.

Kyla had no idea why she did it, but she slipped the

wristband over her injured hand to wear around her wrist brace.

Then from the shoe box she retrieved a smaller box that had once held a child's charm bracelet. Opening that she took out two butterflies he'd made her from foil gum wrappers.

He held out his palm for her to set them in. "I learned how to make those at summer camp when I was nine," he informed her. "Paper crafts. I was surprised I still remembered how to do it."

"I thought you were *so* talented," she said, laughing at what she'd seen as an indication of something greater.

Now, seeing how dwarfed they were in his hand, seeing the thickness of his fingers, the strength and toughness in them, she wondered if he still had the agility.

For that or for the other things he'd done with those hands and fingers…

That's your fault, Darla! Why'd you have to go and make me think even more about that?

"One butterfly was me and one was you," Kyla reminded him.

"We *were* flitting around each other pretty much," he responded.

"Only at first. Then I wouldn't call it flitting—it was more like glued together."

"Every minute we could be," he confirmed with a sentimental smile as she took the butterflies and replaced them in the jewelry box, then put that back in the shoe box, too.

"What is *that*?" he asked, pointing.

"It's an old deflated, dried up, shriveled balloon— it was a dachshund, remember? You bought it for me at that awful music festival you came to with me and my parents—"

"The first time you kissed me—and it *was* you who kissed me!" he said as if there was some kind of victory in that.

"That didn't count—I thought I'd kept you away from the stage through my parents' performance and instead they were just finishing it when we got back. They were doing a song where my father *yodeled*," she said, her voice holding the embarrassment that had caused her then. "I just couldn't think of any other way to keep you from looking in that direction and seeing that that bad music was coming from them."

He laughed. "*That's* why you grabbed my face and yanked me into yours?"

Kyla didn't count that as their first kiss because, while mouths had met, it had been mostly a collision. Plus her eyes had been open, watching the stage she'd turned Beau's back to in order to make sure she didn't let go of him until it was over.

"So you're telling me that our first kiss was nothing but a diversion?" he asked, pretending that news had wounded him.

"That didn't count as the first kiss."

"How do you figure? It was the first time our faces crashed into each other."

"Exactly. And faces crashing into each other can't count as a first kiss. I wasn't even paying attention to it, so nothing registered but keeping you from looking at that stage."

"You might as well not have bothered—your father had been singing those songs the whole week before, while we fixed fences. I recognized the tune, so I knew it was him and your mother up there."

"Really?"

"Really. And if that wasn't our first kiss—"

"It wasn't. The first one was the next night, when we were sitting out on the pier at the lake. When you were trying to persuade me to go skinny-dipping."

He grinned. "Did anybody ever get you to do that?"

"No. But nobody ever tried as hard as you did that night."

"Hard enough to make you so mad that I had to do some fancy footwork to get myself out of trouble."

"Then, when you stopped being a persistent seventeen-year-old jerk—"

"*I* kissed *you*," he said softly, looking at her in a way that told her he remembered it as clearly as she did. That it had meant as much to him. And as their eyes held for a long moment, Kyla was particularly glad that he'd regained the capacity for showing some of his feelings.

Then he nodded down at the box. "I know what all is in there," he said, as if he'd known the whole time.

"No you don't!"

"There's probably the strip of pictures we took in the booth at that diner—minus the one I cut off for myself. There's probably the flyer for the carnival that came through here—you swiped it off one of the lampposts, so I'm figuring you kept it. That carnival was the first time we walked around holding hands."

He was sitting on her left and took her uninjured hand, holding it again the way he had then.

She'd loved the way it had felt fourteen years ago.

And, try as she might, she couldn't help feeling the same way now...

"I'm betting," he went on, "that if I turned the box upside down somewhere in it are the straws we used for that duel we had at the Dairy King when you were still pretending you weren't that into me—I wondered then why you took them with you when we left."

She gave him a look that denied it, but he was right.

"And that finger puppet we were joking around with the night I went babysitting with you," he went on. "When you were still making me work something fierce for every smile but finally gave in and admitted that you liked me. And the napkin I drew the heart on before I had the guts to tell you how I felt out loud. And maybe even the rock? You had to go back to that spot the next day to get the blanket, didn't you? And that's when you found my wristband—when I realized I'd lost it I knew that was where it had to have come off."

He was reading her like a book.

Yes, everything he'd mentioned was in the box. And she *had* gone back to that spot beside the lake.

That spot they'd snuck out to visit on his last night in Northbridge. His birthday. Where they'd spread a blanket because they'd decided to lose their virginities to each other before they had to say goodbye.

"You think you're smart," she said in a quiet voice.

"It's in there, isn't it? The rock that jabbed you in the back when I laid you down? Just after you gave me my birthday present—the marine coin."

He'd taken the rock out from under her so it wouldn't hurt her and set it ceremoniously on the corner of the blanket, telling her as he did that he'd never let anything hurt her.

On that night that had been awkward and clumsy and eventually painful for her anyway.

That night that had been eager and anxious and fretful for him.

And still somehow so sweet...

As much as she didn't want to stop holding hands with him she knew she shouldn't be doing it anyway, so she drew out of his grip in order to rummage around in the box. When she found the rock she showed it to him, laughing a little as she silently conceded that he'd gotten it all right.

Then he reached into his front jeans pocket and took out the coin she'd given him.

She let the rock drop back into the shoe box when he passed her that instead.

She'd been so thrilled when she'd come across it in town shopping for a birthday gift for him. Black and bronze, it had Honor, Courage and Commitment embossed on one side, and the eagle, globe and anchor symbol for the Marines on the other.

Now it was worn almost smooth, the bronze and black faded, the letters and insignia barely visible anymore, especially in the dim glow of the pool lights.

"It's been with me ever since," he said. "Everywhere in the world I've gone. My lucky charm. It always made me think of you."

Why did that cause tears to fill her eyes?

She blinked them away and handed the coin back to him.

He stared at it as he turned it over and over between his fingers, something he'd clearly come to do by habit. "I can't tell you how many times I looked at this when I was home again that year, going back and forth in my mind about what I should do—"

"About the baby?" she asked, alarmed, thinking maybe he'd lied, that he was confessing that he really had known.

He looked at her again, shaking his head. "Just about you," he said, confession in that alone. "I didn't think anything could tear me up the way leaving you did. I told myself it was stupid and that we were just kids and that it couldn't really mean what it felt like it meant, but…"

Another shake of his head. "This coin right here was the whole problem to me—a symbol of the Marines, of what I wanted to be. Given to me by you, the person I wanted to turn my back on everything else for."

Suddenly it was as if all those raw emotions were there, in his face. He really had cared for her the way she'd cared for him, the way she'd thought he did. And she knew without a doubt in that moment that she'd been right all those years ago—had he known about the baby, he wouldn't have left her alone to deal with it. They might even have had the life together that she'd fantasized about.

But it would have cost him his dreams, she reminded herself, realizing it more concretely than she ever had before. Those dreams that had been so important to him.

And maybe that wouldn't have been such a good thing.

What had begun as fun tonight had somehow turned too serious, and Kyla wanted the fun back, so she made a joke of what she now believed was true. "What kind of life would we have had if you had come back to be with me when there was still all that frustrated marine in you? You would have gotten me up at dawn with reveille and put me through calisthenics before making me march through the streets in some kind of formation."

She'd succeeded in lightening the tone again because he laughed, raising his arm to the back of the swing's cushion behind her. "That's not what I was picturing, but it's how it might have ended up," he agreed.

Then he flipped the coin he was still fiddling with with his other hand. "Anyway, this has been my lucky charm," he repeated as he replaced it in his pocket.

Then, with a glint of that wickedness again, he said, "I know it made me lucky that night."

"That was the plan," Kyla said.

"Oh yeah." His voice turned wistful as he reminisced. "Both of us slipping out when everybody else around here was asleep. It was so quiet by the lake that late…the air calm and the smell of wildflowers in it, the grass so cool all around us, the crickets chirping— and there was that frog that kept croaking, remember?"

They both laughed at that, the way they had that night.

Then he looked into her eyes, also the way he had fourteen years ago, and said, "And you were the softest thing I'd ever had my hands on…"

The memory of his hands on her gave her goose bumps.

"There were times when I went back there in my mind," he said, as if that memory had been vital to him. "I hate to think that you probably ended up cursing all of it—and me—instead of thinking about it the way I have. But I'll bet you did, didn't you?"

She was sorry if that tarnished it for him, but still she answered truthfully. "A little. At first I didn't have any regrets. But then I cursed the fact that we were both too afraid of buying condoms," Kyla said drolly.

"Small gossipy town. We weren't even sure they'd sell to a couple of kids. You were worried word would get back to your parents and we wouldn't have our night."

"So we fooled ourselves into thinking that it couldn't happen the *first* time." She rolled her eyes at their adolescent reasoning.

"And since then you haven't thought back on that night the way I have," he concluded.

"Sometimes I have," she admitted, though she didn't tell him that those times had mostly been recently. "Sometimes when I see a clear summer sky it brings back not-so-bad thoughts." The thought of looking up that night at the stars over his shoulder and how much she'd liked the weight of him on top of her...

"You weren't a marine that night," she said, allowing in other, fonder memories of kisses more tentative than they'd been during long make-out sessions, of callused hands that explored with wonder, of stolen peeks at what she knew he'd wanted to study, of care and concern for her comfort, and regret at hurting her.

Beau smiled. "No, I wasn't a marine that night," he agreed. "But you did still make a little of the man in me."

He was looking down into her eyes when the arm behind her curved and came forward so he could brush her cheek with the backs of his fingers.

And whether it was that soft stroke of her face or the mesmerizing effects of his gaze or being back in North-bridge on the ranch with him, there didn't seem to be anything telling Kyla not to tilt her chin up to meet his mouth as it slowly came to claim hers.

There was some of the past in that kiss as it heated up all on its own, as lips parted then went wider, as tongues met again with unveiled eagerness.

Beau reached for the box of mementoes in her lap and dropped it to the ground so he could wrap his other arm around her and pull her closer. And Kyla went will-ingly, letting her own arms creep under his until her hands were on his back once more.

It was quiet. The air was calm. And there were crick-ets chirping in the distance. And Kyla was so lost in kissing Beau that they might as well have been lying on that blanket long ago.

Kissing him was not like kissing anyone else—not anyone before him or anyone since. She didn't know why that was, she just knew that it was true.

Being in his arms wasn't the way it had ever been with anyone else, either. There was just something about it that released her from everything and still gave her a sense of safety and security, leaving her free to go wherever he took her.

And together it all just felt so good, so right to be with him. So much like where she was supposed to be.

He scooped her up and moved her to sit across his lap, as if he needed her closer still. And she went willingly, because being closer to him was what she wanted, too.

She reached up to lay a hand to the side of his neck, going from there to his shoulder, to his biceps, on a quest to experience more of him than she'd gotten to last night.

And it all felt tremendous—rock solid and steely strong without an ounce of excess anywhere.

He didn't seem to have any complaint about being touched because his mouth opened even wider over hers and his tongue play turned more sensuous, more alluring.

She liked knowing she could turn him on. But it wasn't only touching that she discovered she was interested in. The inclination to *be* touched was making itself known.

And not only where he was already touching her. While those big hands felt great on her back, her nipples tightened within the shelf bra that lined her tank top as her breasts began to beg for some attention.

She could take his hand and put it there…

But the kissing was so, so good she also didn't want him distracted. And she didn't want him to know just how badly she was hungering for more.

Then he stopped kissing her mouth and began to kiss her neck, instead. Kissing and sucking lightly and letting just the tip of his tongue do tickly things that created more of those goose bumps.

He kissed a line that led to the hollow of her throat and then along the ridge of her collarbone while she wondered if he was on a path that still might get him where she wanted him to be…

Until he dashed that hope and returned to her mouth.

But there was a new brashness in the way he started kissing her then, something that made it even more sensuous.

And just as she was distracted by trying to figure out how it had changed, one of his hands came to her breast.

It took her off guard and that somehow made it even more exciting, sending her nipple into a tight coil in his palm as his big hand cupped that soft sphere.

It felt so good that a moan escaped her throat even as the thought of skinny-dipping popped into her mind, bringing with it images of skin to skin. Because as nice as it was to have his hand on her breast, there was still too much clothing between them that she wanted gone.

Beau must not have liked the barrier any better than she did because after only a few moments he moved that hand to the hem of her tank top and underneath it for the perfect relocation.

So much better…

His hand was warm, his skin tough and every sensation he brought was blessedly unmuted.

And, oh, the sensations he brought!

No clumsiness, no awkwardness, tonight he was assertive and certain and he reveled in working that mound of flesh, caressing it, kneading it, gently pinching and pulling, tugging and teasing even as his mouth went on plundering hers.

Her injured right hand wasn't good for more than lying flat against his back to keep her anchored, but her left ran rampant over him, too, doing some reveling of her own over hills and valleys of honed muscle.

But still none of it seemed like enough and as she felt the rise of his own need against her hip, she began to recall Darla's peanut butter analogy and think that nothing was going to be enough until she had it all.

Except...

When they were teenagers they'd had a plan. A blanket to cover the ground. The seclusion of the lake in the middle of the night for privacy even out in the open.

Now they were basically in the backyard of his family's home where his brother or sister-in-law could glance through a window and see them. And if they took it inside they'd be in one of the rooms across the hall from the couple.

There was a guesthouse on the opposite side of the pool...

But as Kyla took all things into consideration she realized that she didn't want now what they'd avoided when they were kids—slinking off to merely grope each other.

And despite Darla's advice for her to *get some*—and despite everything in her shouting for her to do that same thing—she wasn't sure she should.

Here, tonight, revisiting the best of their past, she knew that an essence of her younger self had come out, that so had an essence of the younger Beau.

But that wasn't who either of them really was anymore, and she was afraid that letting themselves recapture a piece of that past might end up as a disaster in the light of day.

And disaster was also a part of their past...

So it was thoughts of that old disaster that she hung on to, to subdue the desire running rampant in her and demanding that she just follow her roommate's recommendation. She reluctantly took Beau's hand from her breast at the same time she ended the kissing.

"What are we doing?" she whispered.

Beau didn't answer her, he merely rested his head to the side of hers and let his arm fall across her lap.

"I don't think we better," she added, sounding and feeling like the girl she once was—even when it came to how much she wanted him to ignore her and go back to what he'd been doing.

"I need to be up early and get to the bank and have my driver's license replaced before we can leave in the morning," she went on without any encouragement from him.

Beau finally responded with a nod of his head against hers, accepting the brakes she was putting on things. Unlike the boy he'd once been who would have cajoled and bargained and tried for a little more.

The boy she missed all over again at that moment.

"I can go into town to do that stuff while you give Immy breakfast—if you don't mind."

"Sure," he said, his voice deep and ragged.

"Then we'll drive back?"

He nodded again. But he still wasn't letting go of her. He was still holding her on his lap.

"You said it would take about eight hours?" Kyla said as if nothing else was relevant.

Another nod.

"So we better have four or five bottles, just to be safe."

"I'll take care of it," he said.

Oh, there were so many other things she wanted him to take care of...

But she fought it, fought every inclination she had to kiss him again, to put his hand back on her breast, to just go where everything in her was telling her to go.

Instead she slid off his lap and retrieved the shoe box from the ground along with a couple of things that had spilled out, putting the lid back on it.

And telling herself, as she did so, to put a lid on everything else, too.

Chapter Eight

"Morning."

Beau looked up from feeding Immy her first bottle of the day on Tuesday to answer his brother's greeting. "Hey."

"There isn't usually anybody up before me," Seth said.

Beau nodded but didn't tell Seth that he'd already been up for over an hour, as was normal for him these days.

Seth poured himself a cup of the coffee Beau had made and joined him at the big country kitchen table, nodding at what Beau was doing.

"Looks like you're pretty good at that," Seth observed.

"Not much to it. There's a lot of chance for practice in a day—round the clock—so you get good fast. At this and diapers, too."

"Yeah, not thrilled with the thought of those," Seth grumbled.

"You get used to it," Beau assured him, thinking that he'd seen worse but not saying it.

His older brother stared openly at him while drinking his coffee, then said, "From talking to the family I expected something different from you when you got here."

"Like what?"

Seth shrugged. "I keep hearing that you didn't come back the same. From what I've seen, though, you're a little quieter than you used to be, but otherwise... I haven't noticed you standing around like you're on guard duty or looking like you'd break if you bent over. You *did* knock on the door when you got here—man, does GiGi hate when you do that at home! But you helped yourself to my beer without any problem—" He poked his chin in Beau's direction. "And that right there—you're smiling. How come the family says you never do that? That you're like being around a stone statue of yourself? That's what I was expecting."

Immy had finished her bottle, so Beau sat her on his thigh, braced her chin and chest with one hand and began to pat her back with the other to burp her. "Yeah, being home has been a little rocky," he said as if that answered what his brother had asked.

"Is it better?"

"Getting there."

"This...uh...whole thing with Kyla and Immy. Does that have anything to do with the improvement?"

"Yeah, I think it probably does," Beau admitted. "Seems like babies can break down walls, and Kyla..." He laughed just thinking about her. "Kyla doesn't pull any punches. She's given me some grief about the same things that bother the family. She kind of doesn't let me get away with it."

"And that works because you're pretty hot for her."

Talk about not pulling any punches.

Beau merely gave his older brother a frown that would have made anyone under his command shrink back.

It only made Seth laugh. "Don't try to deny it. Geez, you reek of it! You can't keep your eyes off of her, you get as close to her as you can any time you can, and I saw you out there on the swing with her last night—looking at whatever it was she had in that box, happy as a clam to be doing something that was probably all girly…"

Beau laughed, flashing back to old days of brotherly harassment and just glad that Seth hadn't seen any more than he had of what had happened on the swing last night.

"Hey, you don't have any room to talk—wearing that apron your wife made you wear to barbecue last night. What did it say? Real Men Wear Aprons? I don't think so. What's girlier than an apron?"

Seth grinned but didn't respond to Beau's counterattack. Instead he reached toward Immy and said, "Show me how to hold her so I can practice."

Beau did. Then, with Immy in his brother's care, he went to pour himself a fresh cup of coffee.

When he returned to the kitchen table there was a more serious expression on Seth's face.

"What the old man did wasn't right," he said then. "We all understand what he wrote about not wanting your life ruined, but paying off Kyla's father to make the problem go away? Not letting you know she was pregnant? I heard that she miscarried, but if she hadn't…" Seth shook his head slowly, direly.

"I go to every doctor's appointment with Lacey," he continued. "I have all the ultrasound pictures around the mirror I use when I shave. I can't imagine not even knowing about a kid of mine…not finding out until years later because somebody else decided that's what would be best for me."

There was more head shaking. "You could have had a kid out there in the world and not even known it," he marveled. "How would that have been?"

"Not good," Beau confirmed.

Seth shook his head again, as if he just couldn't comprehend it, and for a moment neither of them said anything.

Then the oldest of the Camden grandchildren said with more caution than he'd started with, "And Kyla… Did you have it as bad for her then as you do now?"

"I was crazy about her," Beau admitted, but only in the past tense.

But his brother persisted. "And now it's just kicked in again?"

Obviously dancing around it was futile, so Beau stopped trying. "I don't know. I don't know whether it's old or new or a combination of the two."

"Does it matter?"

Beau shrugged.

"Are you going to do something about it?" his brother asked.

Beau filled his cheeks with air and blew it out. "Shouldn't."

"Why shouldn't you?"

"For starters it's all pretty confusing between us. It's not like we're coming at it with a clean slate."

"True," his brother conceded.

"And the family's not wrong," Beau went on. "Yeah, I'm in a better mood than I was before I met Kyla again. I guess I've loosened up a little, and it's helped to have more to do, taking care of her and Immy. But…" He shook his head. "I'm not a marine anymore and I'm sure as hell not much of a civilian—feels like I'm in no-man's land. Would you drag somebody else into that?"

"Probably wouldn't be fair," Seth agreed.

"She's helped me figure out what I want to do in Camden Inc—"

"Yeah, Cade told me about that—I think it's a great idea."

"And that's a step."

"A big one," his brother pointed out. "I know you weren't finding anything you wanted to do with us before that."

"But it's still just one step—I haven't actually gone to work, started keeping business hours, put any of it into action. That'll all take a lot. And a lot for me to get into the day-to-day of it."

"Sure, but—"

"And then there's the family and getting to where I fit in again and to where they don't feel like they have to fix me. And that's just the beginning. There's the whole rest of my life—I don't have any vision of that at all at this point. I need to have a distinct direction, a strategy, a course plotted, a firm battle plan—"

"Whoa! Now I'm seeing it!" Seth said to stop him. "You can get intense fast!"

Beau didn't refute that.

"You know, some of life—some of every day—just happens," his brother said then. "You can't have a strategy or a course plotted or a firm battle plan for every minute from now until you're ninety. Nobody can. Lacey and I didn't plan to have this baby—she was a hardcore career woman, juggling working for her father and her own line of clothes and then she added me to the mix, and boom! Birth control failure and we're going to have a kid by the time we hit our first anniversary. Not in the *battle plan*, let me tell you. But so what? That's life. A little surprise can be nice."

"A little surprise in a life that's already pretty stable, Seth," Beau argued. "You've lived in Northbridge and been running this portion of the business since you got out of college. This time three months ago I was in Afghanistan. I knew what I was doing, what was expected of me. Now everything is different and I haven't figured out much of any of it—"

"You bought a house. You're carving out a place in the business—"

"All small steps toward the much bigger picture that's still a blur. And do you think that a relationship would just be another small step in that direction? With someone with her own hands full inheriting a kid and having a business dumped on her? With someone who's spent the last fourteen years hating me?"

"No, but—"

"No is right—that would be throwing a whole can of paint over the top of the blur and making it even worse. And do you think that I'm a prize package when I can't even figure out how to sleep on a civilian's timetable yet? When, out of uniform, I don't know what to wear to a memorial service? When not even GiGi's house feels like home and my own place certainly doesn't? When, yeah, I do stand like a stone statue of myself around people—even family—because I don't know what the hell to talk about?"

Seth's expression was serious again and Beau knew he'd just crushed his brother's hope that the rest of the family was concerned about him for no reason.

Then Seth said, "Okay, so you're not back in the groove. And yeah, there's old stuff with Kyla that carries some weight. But no matter what else is going on with you, Beau, you're good when you're with her. I think that must count for something."

"So you think it's just okay if I use her as a distraction from all this other stuff?"

Seth shook his head. "No. But it doesn't look to me as if that's what you're doing."

"I don't know what I'm doing," Beau said somberly. "And I need to."

Seth's eyebrows arched and he reared back a little. "What *I* think," he responded, "is that we all need to find comfort and support somewhere. Solace. And if you happen across someone who offers that, along the way to figuring everything out, there's no crime in grabbing on to it. Man, I know marines strive for perfection, but you don't have to be the perfect civilian before you can let yourself have some happiness."

"I think I do," Beau said.

"Wow! That was *all* marine," Seth observed, sounding astonished by it. "Are you really that stubborn and bullheaded now?"

"Something else any woman would be thrilled to deal with," Beau said sarcastically.

"Well, cut it out!" Seth shouted the command.

But as good as Beau had become at taking orders, that wasn't one he thought he could execute.

So he merely stared at his older brother.

Knowing that Seth just didn't understand.

"Times like today with Immy give me a new appreciation for quiet," Kyla said when she accepted the glass of wine Beau handed her at ten on Tuesday night.

"Oh yeah," Beau concurred, pouring himself a glass and toasting the air with it for emphasis.

The intended eight-hour drive from Northbridge had taken twelve, and it had been a disaster. Immy had wailed the whole way, never napped, eaten only sporadically, then spewed that onto herself, the car seat and Kyla's car. And if that wasn't enough, there had also been two blow-out diapers that had left Beau cleaning up Immy on the hood of the car while Kyla used baby wipes to one-handedly clean the car seat.

By then Kyla had been in a panic thinking the baby might be seriously ill. Beau had not been able to offer any other perspective and so had gone into emergency mode. Responding calmly and efficiently, he'd used his smartphone to locate the nearest doctor, then driven Kyla's small sedan as if it were an ambulance carrying a critically injured accident victim. They'd rushed into the doctor's office as if the infant were bleeding to death.

Luckily the doctor had been patient with Kyla's anxiety as well as Beau's military-offensive-like invasion of his office. The doctor had checked out Immy, diagnosed car sickness, and told them they were just going to have to tough it out until they got her home.

To the accompaniment of more constant crying, they hadn't accomplished that until after eight o'clock. Once they had the baby out of the car again—as at the doctor's office—she'd seemed fine. So they'd given her a bath, a bottle that she'd taken and kept down, and then Immy had gone peacefully to sleep in her crib.

At that point Beau and Kyla had gone to their separate rooms and bathrooms to shower off the miserable day and were now reconvened in the kitchen for the wine they'd agreed they needed.

"I'm sorry today was so bad," Kyla said then.

"It needed to be done," Beau answered as if it hadn't been as big a deal as it had been.

A different man might have made the bad situations worse by losing his temper. But Beau had been in control through everything. He hadn't seemed affected by the crying as he drove, he'd dealt with the messes without so much as grumbling, and even when Kyla had seen that he was also starting to think there was something seriously wrong with Immy, he'd taken action with complete composure. Maybe too much action, but still, he hadn't been as frantic in the process as Kyla had been. And even now he wasn't complaining.

"I guess the endurance and fortitude you learned in the Marines can come in handy with a carsick two-month-old on a long road trip," she said.

"So *that's* what that training was for," he joked.

Kyla thought it might have been the first time she'd heard him refer to anything military with humor, but she didn't mention that. She just took a sip of her wine and tried to peel her eyes off him.

After his shower he'd come down wearing a form-hugging white T-shirt and a pair of gray sweatpants that rode low on his hips in about the sexiest way she'd ever seen.

"I called the automotive department at the Colorado Boulevard store while you were still upstairs," he said then, obviously unaware of the effect of clothes he'd no doubt put on only for comfort's sake. "I'm having them pick up your car in the morning to clean and detail it inside and out—hopefully that will mitigate some of the damage."

"I didn't know Camden Superstores did that."

"They usually change oil and tires, do some minor repairs."

"But if it's a Camden on the other end of the phone they'll do whatever you ask," Kyla finished for him.

"Rank has its privileges," he said, doing a second air toast before he drank his wine.

And maybe took in the sight of her over his glass while he did, Kyla noticed.

Having brought back her entire wardrobe in the trunk of her sedan, she'd had more clothing options tonight. So after her own shower she'd changed into a flowy navy-blue knit A-line sundress that fell to mid-calf.

She'd chosen it because it was cool and comfortable, and after coming back hot and sticky and splattered with things she hadn't wanted to think about, that had seemed perfect. Plus—like the tank top the night before—the dress had a built-in bra that freed her from wearing anything more constricting.

What hadn't appealed to her was the thought of anything on her feet, so she was barefoot as they stood at the island counter.

They were at a right angle from each other with a bowl of fresh fruit between them that had come straight from the Camden fields in Northbridge. Kyla picked a raspberry out of the bowl to munch.

Then she took a deep breath and said something she'd been avoiding since the day before. "While I was with Darla yesterday I made arrangements for an apartment for Immy and me."

That clearly took Beau by surprise. "In Northbridge?"

"No, I guess it's near here, actually—in a building that overlooks Washington Park?" That was a question rather than a statement because she had no real knowledge of the area—she was only repeating what she'd been told.

"Washington Park isn't far from here," he confirmed, suddenly sounding a little reserved.

"It's Darla's sister Pam's apartment," Kyla explained. "Two bedrooms, one bath, a small kitchen, nothing fancy. There are three months left on the lease and she wants to move in with her boyfriend, so she's been looking for someone to take it over."

Kyla didn't know why this was so difficult to say. Why she couldn't summon even an ounce of enthusiasm for any of it.

Taking over the apartment made perfect sense and it had just fallen into her lap—the ideal solution for her and Immy, and for Darla's sister. Like puzzle pieces fitting into place.

So why didn't it *feel* exactly right? Why wasn't she thrilled with the opportunity to reclaim her independence? Especially when it was being handed to her with so little effort on her part?

She should have been thrilled. And the fact that she wasn't unnerved her.

"Pam—Darla's sister—will leave the place furnished and the kitchen basically stocked because she doesn't need her stuff at her boyfriend's place for now," she went on, not sure if she was elaborating on how perfect it was for Beau's sake or to remind herself. "I'll need to set up a crib and changing table, of course, but I won't need any other furniture." Beau nodded to show he was listening, but didn't say anything.

"At the end of the three months," she continued, "Pam and her boyfriend plan to find a bigger place where both of their things will fit, and she'll take everything then. But in the meantime I can move in with just my clothes and Immy's gear and be all set up. Hopefully at the end of the three months I'll know more about where things stand for Immy and me, and I'll stay and take over the lease, or go back to Northbridge or whatever."

Beau said a clipped, "When?"

"The swelling is down in my fingers and I can move them a little." She demonstrated by raising her right hand and wiggling the no-longer-sausage-like fingers. "And my wrist hurts less and is getting stronger."

"I saw you flinch when you tried to pick Immy up in the car this afternoon," he said matter-of-factly.

"It's better, though. I think another day or two—"

"A day or two," he repeated flatly.

"Then we can be out of your hair, you can have your house to yourself again and go back to normal."

That was met only with silence.

Kyla had no idea why she felt even worse now that she'd told him, now that she'd set the wheels into motion to actually do it. But she did.

"I'll still need your help, though," she said then. "With all the business stuff. That's why—when I told Pam where your house is and she said her place was nearby—I knew it was something I shouldn't pass up. And the rent isn't bad—I wouldn't be able to pay it on my own, but the lawyer said I should start getting the stipend from Rachel and Eddie's estate on the first of the month and that should be more than enough. Plus now I have checks for my own account in Northbridge and the replacement for one of my credit cards was in today's mail."

"Money doesn't matter—"

Kyla laughed, but it was an uncomfortable, forced sound. "Spoken like someone who doesn't live on a tight budget. I'm just saying that the financial predicament I was in right after the fire is resolved. Physically

I'm much better. I *think* I can take care of Immy on my own—as long as I don't try to take her on any long road trips. And staying here was always meant to be just a temporary thing. Until I could get on top of everything. And this week should do it…"

First it was a day or two. Now she was giving herself the rest of the week?

She hadn't wanted to come here in the first place. Why was she dragging her feet about leaving? She should have been rushing out of here. What was wrong with her?

"How did it go so fast?" Beau asked then, as if he was thinking out loud.

The time *had* seemed to fly by, so Kyla had no answer for him.

Then, as if he was reasoning through it all himself, he said, "You do look healthy. Not like that first night I saw you at the motel."

"That's thanks to you—you did all of Immy's nighttime feedings and let me sleep in every morning. You did all the heavy work, all the lifting. You really did let me rest and recuperate, and it paid off."

"So you'll leave and—what? We'll keep in touch?" He said that as if it was a platitude that offended him.

But Kyla answered as if she hadn't noticed. "Sure. Like I said, there's still the truck stops—I haven't even seen the other two of those and don't have any idea how to get to them because I don't know my way around Denver. And I'd rather not take Immy to them by myself, so I'd appreciate help with that. And you said your financial people are working on projections so I'll know whether or not I should take the buyout offer—I thought you'd be with me when that meeting is ready to happen.

And then whatever comes from that—if I need more financial guidance or help running the business or—"

"Right. All the business stuff. I'm still on board for that."

And yet...

There seemed to be some other underlying question that went back to that *we'll keep in touch* comment he'd made.

Then his eyebrows arched a little forlornly and he said, "It just seems so soon. You don't *have* to go, you know? You can stay here the whole time—until you've decided what to do with the business and whether or not to live in Denver or go back to Northbridge."

Oh, sure, spend months here. With him. Things— *something*—was already happening between them in the short time they'd been together. Where might they be months from now?

No, Kyla knew that she had to find a way to get some control over whatever was happening and distance seemed like her only hope of accomplishing that.

"I can't just *stay* here," she said without going into more detail than that.

Beau took an accepting-sounding breath and exhaled, then he nodded in understanding. "I guess it's just been good for me, too," he said. "The place has felt more like home."

"That could be because everything isn't pushed up against a wall and now you have knickknacks to make it feel more homey," Kyla joked, in hopes of easing some of the tension.

"Right—knickknacks. That's probably it," he said facetiously, smiling crookedly at her. Then he seemed to concede. "Just so you know—one or two days, a week, more than that—you can stay as long as you want, it's up to you. And when you are ready to go I'll do whatever you need me to do to help you move and get set up. And even after that…whatever you need."

"Whatever?" she asked leadingly in an attempt to stick to the lighter vein. "You'll come rushing over at three in the morning to kill a spider or empty a mousetrap?"

"Sure."

"How about dirty diaper duty? Can I call and you'll do that?"

He made a face and said with less enthusiasm, "Sure…"

"And where do you stand on babysitting? Let's say, I have a hot date…"

"Not a chance in hell!" he shot back.

"No babysitting? But you'd be perfect for that after all this—Immy knows you, you know how to take care of her."

"I'd babysit. But not for you to go out on a damn date!"

She was just being ornery. She already knew it was going to be even more difficult than before not to compare any man she met to him and find them lacking. Despite the things about him that made her leery, there was still that body, that face, the man himself…

Who was ever going to come close enough to all that for her to consider dating?

And as she stood there, watching him pop a grape into the mouth she'd been missing since the minute she'd made him stop kissing her the night before, looking at that body she wanted to press up against, her conversation with Darla came back into her head.

She wanted Beau so much she could hardly stand it. Regardless of how she tried to fight it, it was still true. Darla was right—he was peanut butter, and once the craving started it didn't stop until she got some. So it did seem possible—likely, even—that unless she satisfied her craving for him, she wouldn't ever be able to move on—not to Pam's apartment, not to other men, not to the rest of her life.

Maybe, she thought, she just had to satisfy the craving and be done with it in order to see straight again…

"I *am* allowed to date, you know," she said then, a flirty challenge in her tone. "There was not a no-dating clause in the guardianship papers."

"I guess I'll see if I can have one added—Camden's has a whole pool of lawyers. With a little underhanded editing you might have to become a nun."

"Never happen. I'm a free agent." Who wasn't exactly sure why she'd chosen this particular back-and-forth with him…

"A free agent with a baby—that could cramp your style," he countered, giving as good as he was getting.

"But Immy is so cute—who won't love her? We'll find someone wonderful and be a little family in no time."

She realized she might have gone too far when he didn't have a quick comeback for that. When, instead, his expression went a little inscrutable before he said, "Don't be mean to me, Gibson."

"I wasn't trying to be," she admitted, sounding once again the way she had when she'd told him about the apartment—shaky.

Then she held out another grape for him as a consolation.

His eyes stuck with hers as he bent over just far enough to take the grape with his teeth, letting the tip of his tongue brush her fingers as he did, then standing straight again.

While he ate the grape he moved with intent around the counter, clasping her arms as he reached to turn her to face him.

Then he leaned forward again and kissed her—a small, simple, enticing kiss that her head tilted back for before she'd even thought about it.

When the kiss ended he said, "You don't need to be up early tomorrow."

It was a reminder of the reason she'd given when she'd stopped things the night before in Northbridge.

"Immy—"

"I take care of Immy then."

"Then *you* have to be up early."

He kissed her again, tracing only the inner edge of her lips with his tongue. And as Kyla drifted away on the way he made her feel, it seemed to cancel everything that had happened between last night and now, and leave her right back where she was then—lost in him...

When that kiss ended he looked intently into her eyes and said sincerely, "Remember how much I wanted you when I was seventeen?"

She did. She'd wanted him as much. So much it had been difficult to breathe just thinking about it.

"A hundred times more right now," he confessed in a gravelly voice.

Kyla closed her eyes and asked herself if she was doing the right thing.

But at that moment it didn't matter.

So she opened her eyes to that beautifully chiseled face and said in a hushed voice, "Me, too."

"It drowns out everything else," he confided.

She nodded.

"But you have to know—"

She didn't know anything other than what was driving her at that moment and before he'd finished his sentence she'd stretched up to silence him with another kiss.

Then, when she ended that kiss, she said, "Just tonight."

His blue eyes searched her face, his brows arched as if to say he wasn't sure about that. But it also seemed as though she'd hit on what he might have been about to say himself because he nodded as if he agreed a split second before his arms came around her.

He pulled her into another kiss that had things heating up instantly as mouths opened wide and tongues were nothing but eager.

So eager they didn't separate even as Beau swept her up into his arms, even as Kyla gasped in surprise and her own arms went around his neck.

He carried her out of the kitchen, down the hall, and when he reached the staircase he took the steps two at a time and went straight for the master suite she'd seen when she helped him choose what to wear to the memorial service.

Once he had her at the foot of his king-size bed he set her on her feet again, mouths still attached and plundering each other with a hunger that seemed to have started long ago and been gaining ground ever since.

He tore his mouth away from hers to cross his arms over his torso and peel his shirt off while Kyla watched.

The plantation shutters on the big bay windows that lined two walls of his room were open, letting moonlight flood in. Milky white light bathed him enough for her to see every muscle and something else—an ugly scar on his shoulder.

She touched it with careful fingertips as if she might hurt him even though it was clearly well healed.

He took her hand and kissed those fingertips. Then he recaptured her mouth with his to ravage all over again.

She rested her still-in-a-brace right hand on the side of his waist while her left hand finally got to have its fill of the feel of his bare skin—sleek and warm. Her fingers glided across his broad shoulder, down his biceps, around to a back that was equally grand and so much better without any shirt to hinder her.

Beau held her face, his thumbs stroking her cheeks before his hands fell to the sides of her neck, then went to her shoulders to massage them in a firm grip.

But only for a while before he hooked fingers under the straps of her dress.

It was loose fitting and all it took to drop to her feet was one sweep of those straps down her shoulders, leaving her wearing nothing but bikini panties in front of him.

Again the kissing stopped so he could blatantly look at her, uttering a sort of guttural growl as his stamp of approval before he spun her around and eased her onto the bed.

From that vantage point she got to look at him again, too, noting that those sweatpants still rode low on his hips before he dropped them and whatever was underneath them.

Wow.

She might have seen him naked years ago. She might have done a lot of studying and ogling of him since she'd been here. But nothing was like the unrestricted view as he undressed now.

"Oh, Camden, how you've grown…" she muttered, making room for him on the mattress without taking her eyes from the feast in front of her.

He laughed wickedly as his own gaze took her in once more, too, and his expression—and other substantial parts of him—showed his appreciation.

Then he joined her on the bed, lying beside her to kiss her again, one hand resting lightly on her stomach.

But that wasn't where she wanted it and she was only too glad when it rose to find her breast.

She'd been reliving his touch since she'd left him poolside on Monday night and still that first sensation took her breath away. Plus the years had taught him skills that made it impossible for her not to melt under the hand that knew precisely when to be soft and gentle, when to be firm and just a little rougher. When to circle her nipple with the lightest of strokes. When to tug and tenderly pinch, every bit of it making her want even more.

All while she did her own touching, her own rejoicing in the freedom to finally have her hands on what she'd been studying for what seemed like ages. On what felt even better than it looked and fed the desire in her with every inch she explored.

The man was just magnificent everywhere and she reveled in it. Back and shoulders and arms and pectorals and abs of iron. Thighs front and back, and oh, that derriere!

His mouth deserted hers then, to kiss her neck, to nibble and nudge and do tiny tongue-flicks on an excruciatingly slow path to her other breast.

But he stalled before he went as far as she wanted him to go and instead merely placed a scant kiss to the upper swell. He brushed that same spot with his nose, teasing her with hesitation so the yearning would grow.

So that when he finally went those few inches lower, when he finally kissed her breast once a little farther down, a second time a little farther down, a third time just on the very outer edge of her nipple before he did take her breast into his mouth, it felt so good her spine arched and drew her off the mattress in precious agony.

But once he put his mouth to work it was a heaven of hot, moist torment that nearly drove her wild.

Wild enough to dig her fingers into that very fine derriere of his.

But somehow she knew that that wasn't exactly where he wanted her hand, and by then it wasn't where she wanted it, either.

A little retaliation seemed only fair, though, so she drew that hand to his hip very slowly, doing small strokes there with only her fingertips, lingering until he gave her a little nip accompanied by a guttural groan of complaint to let her know she was torturing him.

Which made her smile even as he sucked her breast far, far into his mouth and turned her on even more.

Enough to stop toying with him and reach for him.

Not the boy she remembered.

Fabulously all man now—long and hard and so thick.

The sound he made when she first touched him let her know she'd granted his wish and the heat went up from there.

Not only was there more intensity in his mouth at her breast, but his hand trailed down her stomach again, diving between her legs and into her in one smooth motion.

Oh…definitely more skills…

There was preview in what he was doing and it again stole her breath and arched her spine.

It just wasn't enough.

So she tightened her hand around him and slid a little up and down, up and down…

Then his control snapped.

He rolled away from her, out of her reach, opening the drawer on one of his nightstands and grabbing for protection that he applied in a hurry.

He rolled back when he had and his mouth was on hers again, open wide, ravishing, his tongue there and not, elusive and aggressive, as that divine body came over her, fitting himself between her thighs, teasing her with more than his fingers now.

But Kyla couldn't wait any longer to have him. She spread her knees wider in invitation and that was when he slipped into her, making her moan this time as he went just slowly enough, slow and steady, until he was all there.

Kyla felt her muscles tighten around him as if to keep him within her forever, but still he slid partway back, then in again, insistent but careful, easing himself into her, retreating, picking up speed in measured paces.

But still the speed came and Kyla met and matched it, her arms around him, her eyes closed as she was carried away by sensation, by the feel of him inside of her, by what he was awakening, nurturing, making grow and rise.

And then what hadn't happened for her that first awkward time happened now, and he took her to a peak higher than she'd ever reached. So high she couldn't do anything but push up into him, frozen, immobile, seized in the grip of something so incredible she didn't even need to breathe, something so amazing she gave herself over to it—to him—completely, trusting him to make it last and last and last...

And last it did, blissfully long, engulfing her, consuming her in a way she never wanted to end.

Then, just as it began to, he plunged even deeper into

her and reached that same peak himself. Strong and unyielding above her, most of his weight gloriously on top of her, letting her feel what was happening to him.

She curled her legs over his, reached for his rear end again and drew him in deeper still, holding him there until his entire body shuddered with relief. Until muscle by muscle started to let up, to relax, to make him heavier and heavier on top of her.

For a moment they stayed like that and Kyla savored it—trying to absorb every detail, every nuance, every inch of where his body met hers.

Then weakness finally made her legs fall from around his to the mattress and he took some of his weight onto his arms again to raise his upper half above her and lay his forehead to the top of her head.

"Did I hurt you this time?" he asked in a passion-gravelly voice.

She smiled. "Not even once."

"Good," he said on a replete sigh, clearly worried that he might have.

She was sorry when he slipped out of her but happy again when he'd cleaned up and returned to pull her to lie close against his side, to use the hollow of his shoulder as a pillow.

"I can't believe I'm saying this after months of insomnia, but I need to sleep," he said with a laugh then.

"I'm a tranquilizer?" she joked.

"Oh, you're so much more than that..." he moaned. "And I need more of it, if you'll just give me a little rest first."

"And if I say no?" She drew a circle around his nipple, watching it tighten not quite as impressively as hers did.

He laughed, a very sexy rumble from deep in his chest. "I'll try to oblige you."

"But if you rest?"

"You won't be sorry," he promised, hugging her closer.

"Maybe just a *little* nap then," she said, looking up at him once more.

But for some reason seeing the softness of his smile, the lines of that masculine face in pure tranquility, flooded her with feelings.

Feelings that terrified her.

Feelings that she couldn't—wouldn't—give in to.

So she closed her eyes and let the exhaustion pull her away from them and back into her own serenity there in his arms.

Dodging all the emotions that had threatened, she just immersed herself in the physical feelings that were too good to let go of.

Chapter Nine

"Hey, little girl, you're making a lot of noise," Beau said softly as he reached the side of Immy's crib at sunrise on Wednesday.

Seeing him, hearing his voice, the infant went from crying to a whimper and then she put her fist in her mouth to suck on it, letting him know she was hungry.

Or at least that was how Beau read it.

By now they had an early morning routine—she seemed to know that when he came into the room the bottle wasn't far behind, so she usually quieted while he changed her diaper, pacifying herself with the fist sucking.

Even so, he made sure to be quick with the diaper change, then he took her with him downstairs to heat her bottle. Once he was ready to feed her he went somewhere to sit—sometimes at the breakfast nook, sometimes in the family room, sometimes outside.

Today he took Immy and the bottle back up to the nursery and sat in the rocking chair.

Any other day he would have been up for an hour or two before her. He would have taken the baby monitor with him to his workout room so he could hear her if she started to cry before he was finished putting himself through his paces. Some mornings, after her bottle and a good burping, Immy fell back to sleep and if she did that and left him with nothing to do, he took her with him back to his basement gym to do another workout while she snoozed on a blanket on the floor nearby.

But today was different.

For the first time he'd had to drag himself out of bed both for the 2:00 a.m. feeding and for this one.

And he was hoping Immy would fall back asleep so he could return her to her crib and go back to his own bed.

Where Kyla was.

Sitting in the rocker, he positioned Immy in the crook of his left arm and offered her the bottle. She took it, peacefully settled into eating, and he rested his head against the back of the chair and closed his eyes.

If he gave in to it, he could be asleep again himself in minutes. He hadn't felt like that since he'd been discharged and it was nice.

But if he made it back to bed it wasn't more sleep he was actually looking forward to. He had high hopes for round four of making love to Kyla...

Just the thought of her, of the night they'd had together, of the possibility that it might not have to be over, made him smile. And for a minute he let himself bask in a very real sense of calm and contentment that he hadn't experienced in longer than he could remember. It was what he'd expected to feel being home again but hadn't been able to achieve. Until now. With Kyla.

Kyla, who had told him she was moving out...

He opened his eyes. And there was no more smiling.

He hadn't thought about what Kyla had told him since they'd gone on to the other—much, much better—things last night. But now there it was, hitting him all over again the way it had hit him when she'd said it—like a roadside bomb almost as big as the news that she'd been pregnant fourteen years ago.

She was mostly well again and she was leaving.

And recalling that made something rip through him that was worse than shrapnel.

She was leaving.

He was going to lose her again—that had been his first thought last night when she'd told him about her friend's apartment, and that was what he thought again now.

Leaving...

Like he'd left her.

When other things had fallen into play and fourteen damn years had happened and they'd been lost to each other that whole time.

Trying to stay grounded, he reminded himself that she wasn't disappearing off the face of the earth. That she would be nearby. That he was still signed on to help her with Immy's inheritance—a built-in reason to go on seeing her. And Immy, too.

But it didn't make it any better.

It didn't even make it better when he told himself that there wasn't anything that said he couldn't keep in touch beyond business, that they couldn't date.

Because he was beyond wanting to merely *date* Kyla.

And because of that damn joke she'd made the night

before about him babysitting for Immy while she dated somebody else...

Yeah, that had hit him hard, too, joke or no joke.

The thought of her with some other guy?

It had been bad enough hearing about the men she'd kept company with between her time with him that summer and now. At least none of it had panned out and he hadn't had to watch it.

But thinking about her with anyone else now, thinking that she might get serious with someone, start a future with them, was torture.

And dammit, being relegated to just dating her himself felt like a demotion after living together, caring for a child together.

Their time together had already been more concentrated. As it had been that summer. Isolated. Insulated in a way that had made it more personal, more private. Only about them.

How could he go from that to just seeing her by prearranged appointments? To *dating* her, when they already had so much more than that?

He was in a tailspin and he tried to stop it by asking himself what else he was going to do. She was right— she *was* a free agent. And no, she probably couldn't just stay here forever.

Plus, only yesterday morning he'd told his brother that it wasn't fair to bring anybody into his life before he had everything worked out. His job, his future, himself. That things needed to be in better shape before he could even think about bringing a relationship into the mix. Especially when Kyla was in so much upheaval herself. And given their history.

All of that was true. Absolutely true. Every bit of it.

But up against the thought of her leaving?

None of it mattered. He only cared about her leaving. So what was he going to do?

Seth had said that he didn't have to be the perfect civilian before he could have some happiness. Beau had shot that down. But now he considered it.

He was nowhere near to being the perfect civilian, that was for sure. But as he thought about it, he realized that Kyla had helped him get a little closer.

Thanks to her he had a job to do within Camden Incorporated now, which meant that he could finally go to work. That would put structure and purpose into every day and finally start him on a civilian track that didn't make him feel like a slacker.

His family seemed to breathe a sigh of relief at the job placement, too, and he thought that would go a long way in making them stop worrying about him. And with the common ground they all had now, he hadn't seemed so much like an outsider on Sunday and hopefully things would build from there.

No, nothing had been implemented yet, nothing was on a firm course, but at least he had some direction. And while he might not be in the shape he'd been demanding of himself, he decided that he was in better shape than he'd thought.

But was it good enough to try for more with Kyla?

Kyla, who had a lot on her own plate.

Who had spent the last fourteen years thinking he was a dirtbag.

Who seemed uncomfortable with the idea of raising Immy with the structured schedules his background had trained him to provide.

He wasn't sure.

There was last night…

But he had no way of knowing if that had been the

same thing it was when they were teenagers—a way of saying goodbye.

Something clenched inside him all over again at that thought.

It had been bad enough leaving her behind fourteen years ago, and there was so much more to her now.

Warm and kind and caring. Thoughtful and strong and smart and funny. Sometimes tough on him—just the way he liked it.

She was Kyla from the past, but refined and improved with the girl in her still there to tease him and call him on anything that he needed to be called on. She had the power to loosen him up when nothing else could. The capacity to make him relax more than he'd been able to since he'd been discharged, more than he'd been able to even before that. She softened his rough edges. She made him feel things that no one before her or since her had. Kyla and Immy, too.

And finding Kyla again was what had truly brought him home.

How could he let any of that go?

He looked down at Immy to gauge her progress on the bottle, wondering as he did if maybe H.J. had stepped in and changed what hadn't been meant to be changed.

Because here they were, where they'd left off—complete with a baby the way it might have been then—and this was what felt right.

He wanted Kyla in his life no matter what shape that life was in or where it was headed.

He wanted Immy in his life—because staring down at her and thinking about someone else coming in and loving her, raising her, hurt as much as the thought of another man with Kyla.

They were his. His girls. And that was all there was to it. Whether his life was perfect or imperfect. Whether the timing was right or not. Regardless of how scarred the past might be.

They were his. Here and now.

That was just how it had to be.

It *had* to be.

He closed his eyes again, letting his conclusions sink in.

And hoping to God that Kyla felt the same way he did.

Groggy and heavy-lidded, Kyla made it as far as the nursery door and silently deflated against the jamb, anchored there by the heaviness of not nearly enough sleep. Of hardly any sleep, really.

On any other night she wouldn't have been in Beau's room to hear Immy's cries over the monitor, so she would have gone right on sleeping through them. But being in his room all night had kept that from happening. Plus there had been other things occupying her time that hadn't involved sleep.

She'd wanted to get up for the 2:00 a.m. feeding, but Beau had nixed the idea. What he'd wanted—he'd said with her naked body molded to his, his arms around her and after kissing the top of her head—was for her to conserve her energy until he got back.

She'd conserved it, but she hadn't slept and instead had arranged herself in his bed so that she could again watch him shed his sweatpants once Immy was fed and taken care of. What had followed was their second session of lovemaking, about an hour of talking and joking and teasing afterward, then more lovemaking. And altogether that lack of sleep, coupled with all the…exertion, had left her tired. A good tired, but tired nonetheless.

It *was* morning now, though—however early—so after Beau had again slipped on his sweatpants and left the room, she'd fought back and forth with sleep for awhile then gotten out of bed, too.

She'd spotted him across the hall in the nursery when she'd left the master suite, but now that she'd reached Immy's room she gave in to yet another indulgence— since he was facing just enough away from the door not to have seen her, she rested against the jamb to watch him without announcing herself.

Only a hint of the sunrise's pale pink-and-orange glow came in through the nursery windows, casting just enough light for her to see his chiseled face and the scruff that shadowed his sculpted jawline as he gazed down at the baby and the bottle that his big hand dwarfed as he held it for her.

Once more he had on only his sweatpants, leaving his feet and his upper half bare. Immy nestled comfortably against his lean abs, gently cradled in arms as thick as tree branches.

And they looked so comfortable with each other. So accustomed to each other. So much as if they belonged together…

But that kind of thinking was something she knew she *shouldn't* indulge in, so she pushed away from the doorjamb and went the rest of the way into the nursery.

That movement caught Beau's attention and he looked up at her with those blue, blue eyes, taking her in from tousled hair to his T-shirt to bikini panties that peeked from under it to bare legs and feet.

It would have been as easy to put on her dress again when she'd gotten out of bed—it was on the floor along with his T-shirt. And the dress would have been more concealing. Or she could have gone into her own bed-room for her robe.

But it was his T-shirt that she'd wanted wrapped around her. The clean, soapy scent of him making her feel as if it was still him next to her skin.

He smiled a smile that made her blood rush—full of warmth and appreciation and that devilishness he kept so well concealed most of the time.

"You're just who I wanted to see," he whispered.

"Oh, yeah?" she whispered back impishly as she came to stand near the rocking chair to peer down at Immy.

Immy was so cute with her coppery curls and her chubby cheeks. Her eyes were closed as she finished her bottle, a tiny fist just under the side of her chin. Kyla couldn't help reaching out to brush the baby's brow, moving close enough to Beau for her leg to press against his, again making herself a part of what they were sharing.

"I think she's done," Kyla whispered then, because Beau was looking at her and not at Immy. Then she reached for the bottle as he drew it out of Immy's still-suckling mouth so he could raise the swaddled bundle to his shoulder to pat a burp out of her.

It only took a minute and it was loud enough to make them both smile, then Beau lowered Immy again—apparently to see if she was sleeping.

She was and he said, "Thank you, Immy," as if he and the baby had made some kind of deal.

Then he got up from the rocking chair and put her in the crib.

"She goes back to sleep now?" Kyla asked.

"Not always. But I was hoping she would today."

With Immy settled—and without another sound—he took Kyla's hand to lead her out of the nursery.

Following him she ogled the magnificence of his naked back, thinking that she knew what was on his mind and that the same thing was on hers—returning to his bed to make love yet again.

But once they were in the master suite he didn't go all the way to the bed. Instead he spun her around and loosely draped his arms around her, his hands clasped at the small of her back.

"Marry me, Kyla," he said, no longer whispering.

Kyla laughed because he had to be kidding. "Sure," she said facetiously.

"I mean it."

There was something in his voice that confirmed that and sobered her.

She frowned up at him in confusion. "What?"

"I want you to marry me," he said matter-of-factly. "I know I don't have the civilian stuff under control yet and I need a better handle on it all, but I think I have a start and I know I'll get there because I won't let up on myself until I do."

He went on to tell her what had gone through his mind since he'd left her in bed.

Some of it was wonderful and touched her and tempted her.

But more of it pushed panic buttons in her.

"When Seth said maybe I didn't have to wait until I'm the perfect civilian to be happy," he seemed to be concluding, "I blew it off, but—"

"So being a civilian again is a hill you need to conquer and I'm the troops you want to command to do it," she cut him off, translating what that had sounded like to her. "With what? Schedules and organization and timetables like you laid out when Immy and I first got here?"

Even as the words flooded out of her she knew she wasn't handling this well. But everything that made her worry about getting involved with him, everything she'd cautioned herself about, had flooded into her mind at once while he'd talked and it threw her off balance. So off balance that she eased out of his arms and took a few steps away from him as if distance was her only hope of regaining her equilibrium.

"Well, yes and no," he said, looking surprised by her response. "Getting used to being a civilian is something I need to conquer, and yeah, I like schedules and organization and the rest of that. I think we all need discipline and rules to follow. But was I figuring I'd be in *command* of you? That I'd be telling you what to do? No. In case you haven't noticed, you don't take orders all that well."

"So there would be a constant tug-of-war between us—that wouldn't be good," she argued.

His brows dipped toward the bridge of his nose. "I don't feel like we have a constant tug-of-war."

"But we're different, Beau. A lot different. That's what comes out of that. I'm not the way my parents were, but I'm more like them than like you—"

"Who says we have to be alike? I think our differences even us out. You kick the starch out of me, and you said that after growing up the way you did you wanted a little structure—"

"A *little* structure—"

"And if I step over the line trying to put more in than you want, you stop me."

"But what does that mean? That we'll have a whole life of me having to stop you from stepping over lines?

My parents were fruitcakes in their own way, but they were the same kind of fruitcakes—they wanted the same things, had the same goals, the same dreams, they agreed on things, they were both okay with the way they lived. They were *alike*, so they never fought. I don't think anyone has a chance of making it work if it means an entire future of struggling to find common ground—"

"We might not be as alike as your parents were, Kyla, but we don't *struggle* over everything, either. I think we're pretty good at bringing our own strengths to the table and finding a compromise. Isn't that better than the way your parents were together? Better than no one knowing when to put on the brakes or be responsible or take care of their kid or do the grocery shopping?"

He was arguing with logic, but this had all thrown her and fear was her fuel.

"I don't know if it's better or not," she said. "But I do know that I can't just be your underling—"

He laughed with a hint of wickedness tingeing his own confusion. "There are some advantages to being under me some of the time," he joked. But when he saw that she was in no way in a joking mood, he sobered again.

"I can't—I *won't*—raise Immy in boot camp," she said as if he wasn't seeing her point of view.

"And what would you do if I even unconsciously fell into doing that?" he asked, sounding rational and sensible.

"I'd blow you right out of the water!" she threatened defensively.

"Exactly. You wouldn't let it go on and when you blew me out of the water it would open my eyes to what I was doing and I'd stop it. Because I agree with you—

kids shouldn't be raised like that. I promise you, Kyla, I'm not talking about being commander-in-chief here. I'm talking about a partnership. And I've never known you not to be able to hold your own with me—you have an independent streak that's a mile wide. I admire that. I like it. I wouldn't want you to change."

"But marriage sacrifices some of that independence. It's risky…" And it would mean trusting him and a future with him.

He must have read what she was thinking in her face because he said, "I'm sorry you were hurt all those years ago, Kyla. I'm so damn sorry. But you weren't wrong to believe in me then and you can trust me now."

"And what about *then*?" she demanded. "Is this coming from guilt about what happened when we were kids? Because you can't base a lifetime on that, Beau. If you think you're just stepping up a little late—"

"Wow, you are spinning, aren't you? I would do anything—*anything*—to wipe out what happened then. To change it. To have it to do over again. But none of that's possible. And the only thing that then and now have to do with each other is that you're who I fell in love with then, and who I've fallen in love with all over again. This isn't about the past, it's about the future. It's about you and me, and me wanting you in my life."

He took a step to close some of the distance between them but still left her breathing room—as if he knew she needed it. He reached out to clasp her upper arms in those big hands as he said, "I *love* you, Kyla. I will do *whatever* it takes to make you happy because you make *me* happy. I will do whatever it takes to make this work now because I want it to work now, and not because of anything that came before. We were kids and that was first love and maybe that's where what we have now is rooted, but the roots are only the beginning—this is more than that…so much more. And when it comes to Immy…"

He shook his head as if in awe of his own feelings. "I love Immy, too," he said. "I know she isn't ours, but if my great-grandfather and your father hadn't done what they did, a baby would have brought us together a long time ago. And now a baby brought us together again. Maybe that's because this is the way it was meant to be all along. That's sure as hell how it feels to me."

And it was such a nice way of looking at it.

But still…

"I don't know. I don't know. I don't know…" Kyla lamented, wanting to let herself be swayed. Wanting to just get back into that bed with him.

But this was all coming at her too fast. Too unexpectedly. And so early in the morning. After a night when she'd had very little sleep. And she was having trouble thinking straight. Trouble doing anything but reacting to what were hot-button issues for her.

Immy let out a half cry just then and they both glanced in the direction of the nursery.

"I'll get her," Kyla said with more urgency than the scant cry called for because she wanted—needed—an escape.

But Beau vetoed it. "You shouldn't lift her. I'll check on her and give you a minute," he said softly, taking his hands away.

She didn't argue, she just watched him go and then collapsed on the edge of the bed as if the wind had been knocked out of her.

Fourteen years ago, as a pregnant sixteen-year-old, she'd fantasized about Beau proposing to her. Dreamed of it.

Now it just scared her.

And it certainly wasn't what was supposed to have come out of making love with him last night! That was supposed to have put an end to her craving for him so she could move on.

But it hadn't put an end to the craving. It had actually only made it worse.

He *was* chocolate, not peanut butter.

And she never got enough chocolate…

But he also wasn't the seventeen-year-old semi-man he'd been in those early fantasies and dreams. Now he was tougher. He was a force. He was all marine.

Being more like her parents than like him, Kyla knew that made her almost the opposite end of the spectrum. And no, she didn't want a life of tug-of-war, of struggling, of holding the line against the marine.

Except that that wasn't what it felt as though she'd been doing. Without him standing right in front of her, she thought about this time they'd spent together since he'd shown up at the truck stop.

There had been a bit of a tug-of-war between them at first. Over his schedules and him wanting her to nap and other details of the course he'd plotted for what he thought was the best way to deal with their situation.

But when she'd balked, when she'd made the corrections to it that she'd wanted to make, he'd accepted them without a problem. The same way he'd accepted the changes she'd made to his house. And every change that had needed to be made along the way with Immy.

All without any kind of real struggle.

He liked to have a plan, but if varying from the plan was called for, he did it. He adapted. So while he gave the impression that he might be inflexible, he wasn't really.

And if she had any doubts she had only to think about their awful drive home from Northbridge with a carsick two-month-old when his plans to drive straight through had turned into such a disaster. He'd rolled with the whole thing. Without showing any kind of frustration or annoyance. Without complaint.

It was really himself that he was hardest on, she realized. He expected and demanded more of himself than he did of anyone else. But when she thought about it, she realized that he hadn't made any demands on her. He hadn't expected anything of her. To her he'd been considerate, caring, attentive and always concerned with her health, her needs. He would have waited on her hand and foot if she'd have let him.

And he'd said that she helped loosen him up, helped him relax. She could admit that she'd seen that happening. So really he'd done more changing to accommodate her than she'd done to accommodate him.

Not that she hadn't done *any* adapting to him. When he was right he was right, and she'd gone along with his suggestions. He was right about trying to keep Immy on a regular schedule, and he was more able than Kyla was to take things a step at a time to get on top of them when she was on the verge of buckling beneath too much at once.

Kind of like now...

But then that made him right now, too, didn't it? she asked herself. They did each bring something different to the table. And they were pretty good at compromising.

That give-and-take *was* better than her parents being two peas in a pod. That had been nice for them, but it certainly hadn't been responsible or efficient. And it had left their child fending for herself.

There was nothing about that that she wanted for Immy.

Actually, when she considered the pattern she'd

fallen into with Beau for caring for Immy, it struck her that they did work as a team, as partners—Kyla did whatever she could, Beau did whatever she couldn't, until everything was taken care of and so that nothing important was overlooked or forgotten.

That seemed like a pretty good way to handle parenting. And they were pretty good at it…

He was logical and he looked at things in a stripped-down sort of way that helped deal with problems. Certainly he'd done that for her own situation with becoming a single parent, with needing to oversee the truck stops, so why should she think that he wouldn't do that if other kinds of problems arose?

And he listened to her. He respected her opinions, her views. He took her seriously. He didn't just disregard her or anything she said. So if they disagreed, it seemed like they'd still be able to hash it out.

And it was kind of good to know that he could keep his head when she lost hers a little…

Kind of good to know, but had she already come to rely too much on him? she asked herself, rattled by that idea.

She'd been relying on his help with Immy—but only for things she was incapable of doing and only temporarily.

She was relying on his guidance when it came to Immy's inheritance—but that, too, would only be until she got sound advice on what to do and had learned what she needed to know to do it all herself.

What she was considering now went so much further than either of those things.

And it wasn't temporary…

Was she willing to put herself in a position where she regularly relied on someone else? Where she had to trust that he was the person she thought he was and wouldn't let her down?

That was a big leap for her...

She hadn't even had parents she could trust or rely on.

But who was more trustworthy than Beau? she asked herself now.

She did believe that if he'd known she was pregnant he would have come through for her all those years ago. And he'd come through for her now—despite the resentment and anger and accusation she'd thrown at him at first.

Plus she knew he was all about honor and respect and responsibility and doing what was right—if she could rely on anyone it was him.

She looked through the open bedroom doors to where Beau was leaning over the crib. He was gently rubbing Immy's back to soothe her.

And just that sight of him told Kyla what she needed to know.

She loved him. She loved him with all the passion she'd had when she was sixteen. But, unlike when she was sixteen, what she felt for him now had more depth, more dimension. And it was with her eyes wide open.

So if it meant some compromise, if it meant some tug-of-wars down the road, if it meant giving up a little of her independence—no matter what it meant—it didn't matter.

She wanted him.

She wanted to be with him.

She wanted to raise Immy with him.

And she wanted Immy to have him, too, because she knew that he would be the best thing she could ever give her tiny new charge to make up for losing her own parents.

The breath Kyla took then felt as though it washed away all the debris of her fears and concerns and left her—finally, fully—able to embrace the thought that this man, who she truly loved, had asked her to marry him.

She stood up again, went into the nursery and took Beau's hand the same way he'd taken hers before, leading him away from the dozing-again Immy and back to the master suite.

There she also did what he'd done—she stopped and turned to face him, letting go of his hand in hopes that he'd put his arms around her again.

But he didn't. He stayed still, giving her space.

"I'm sorry," she said into that space, looking up into his eyes as his brows shot up.

She could see that he thought she was beginning the big No and she raised a hand to his chest as she said, "I'm sorry I went a little crazy. You surprised me."

That was such an oversimplification and she thought he probably knew that, so she went on to explain what she'd had to work through to get where he already was.

He listened patiently and when she was finished she said, "I do love you, Beau. More than it seems like anybody should love anybody. I guess I've been trying to make my feelings into something else, into something that didn't run as deep as they do, but I was just fooling myself. Maybe I was fooling myself for the whole fourteen years since—"

He breathed a sigh of relief and pulled her to him. "Just say you'll marry me."

"I will," she said without hesitation.

"Soon. Because we've already waited long enough,"

he added, wrapping his arms even more tightly around her so that her cheek was pressed to his chest.

"Soon," she confirmed, sliding her arms around him, too, and hanging on, thinking how nice it was to have him to hang on to.

"And I'm never letting you go again," he said, mirroring what she was feeling.

"Good," she answered with a little laugh, "because I'm counting on that and it isn't easy for me to count on anybody."

"Yeah, I've noticed," he said, holding her even tighter.

Immy started to fuss again and Kyla moaned. "I was kind of hoping she might stay asleep so we could——"

"Me, too," Beau said. "Doesn't look like she's going to, though. We'll just have to shoot for her next nap."

"Do marines go back to bed during the day?" she goaded him.

"This one does today," he said with that tinge of evil that made her smile.

She tipped her head back far enough to peer up at him again. "And you're sure you want the whole package— with baby making three?"

"I would have been sure fourteen years ago and I'm sure now. For some reason it just seems to be the way fate wants us to start out. And I'm more than okay with that," he said just before he dipped his head down far enough to kiss her—a poignant, profound kiss that she gave herself over to possibly more than any that had come before.

But Immy was insistent now and the kiss couldn't go on as long as Kyla wanted it to.

In spite of the racket the baby was making, though, Beau still spent another moment holding her, pressing her head to his chest again, kissing the crown of her head.

"You're my girls," he said then, his voice full of emotion. "And nobody else's."

Kyla kissed the big chest she seemed to fit against so perfectly and decided that regardless of how much of her independence might go by the wayside, it was worth it to have this man.

This very special man who she would never stop being grateful for.

Who she would never stop loving.

Who she knew would be hers for the rest of her life.

* * * * *

COMING NEXT MONTH FROM

HARLEQUIN®

SPECIAL EDITION

Available February 17, 2015

#2389 MENDOZA'S SECRET FORTUNE
The Fortunes of Texas: Cowboy Country • by Marie Ferrarella
Rachel Robinson never counted herself among the beauties of Horseback Hollow, Texas...until handsome brothers Matteo and Cisco Mendoza began competing for her attention! But it's Matteo who catches her eye and proves to be the most ardent suitor. He might just convince Rachel to leave her past behind her and start life anew—with him!

#2390 A CONARD COUNTY BABY
Conard County: The Next Generation • by Rachel Lee
Pregnant Hope Conroy is fleeing a dark past when she lands in Conard County, Wyoming, where Jim "Cash" Cashford, a single dad with a feisty teenager on his hands, resides. When Cash stumbles across Hope, he's desperate for help, so he hires the Texan beauty to help rein in his daughter. As the bond between Cash and Hope flourishes, there might just be another Conard County family in the making...

#2391 A SECOND CHANCE AT CRIMSON RANCH • by Michelle Major
Olivia Wilder isn't eager for love after her husband ran off with his secretary, leaving her lost and lonely. So when she scores a dance with handsome Logan Travers at his brother's wedding, her thoughts aren't on romance or falling for the rancher. A former Colorado wild boy, Logan is drawn to Olivia, but fears he's not good enough for her. Can two individuals who have been burned by love in the past find their own happily-ever-after on the range?

#2392 THE BACHELOR'S BABY DILEMMA
Family Renewal • by Sheri WhiteFeather
The last thing Tanner Quinn wants is a baby. Ever since his infant sister died, the handsome horseman has avoided little ones like the plague—but now he's the guardian of his newborn niece! What's a man to do? Tanner calls in his ex-girlfriend Candy McCall to help. The nurturing nanny is wonderful with the baby—and with Tanner, too. Although this avowed bachelor has sworn off marriage, Candy might just be sweet enough to convince him otherwise.

#2393 FROM CITY GIRL TO RANCHER'S WIFE • by Ami Weaver
When chef Josie Callahan loses everything to her devious ex-fiancé, she leaves town, hightailing it to Montana. There, Josie takes refuge in a temporary job...on the ranch of a sexy former country star. Luke Ryder doesn't need a beautiful woman tantalizing him—especially one who won't last a New York minute on a ranch. He's also a private man who doesn't want a stranger poking around...even if she gets him to open his heart to love!

#2394 HER PERFECT PROPOSAL • by Lynne Marshall
Journalist Lilly Matsuda is eager to get her hands dirty as a reporter in Heartlandia, Oregon. The locals aren't crazy about her, though—Lilly even gets pulled over by hunky cop Gunnar Norling! But the two bond. As Gunnar quickly becomes more than just a source to Lilly, conflicts of interest soon arise. Can the policeman and his lady love find their own happy ending in Heartlandia?

YOU CAN FIND MORE INFORMATION ON UPCOMING HARLEQUIN® TITLES, FREE EXCERPTS AND MORE AT WWW.HARLEQUIN.COM.

HSECNM0215

REQUEST YOUR FREE BOOKS!

2 FREE NOVELS PLUS 2 FREE GIFTS!

♦ HARLEQUIN®

SPECIAL EDITION

Life, Love & Family

YES! Please send me 2 FREE Harlequin® Special Edition novels and my 2 FREE gifts (gifts are worth about $10). After receiving them, if I don't wish to receive any more books, I can return the shipping statement marked "cancel." If I don't cancel, I will receive 6 brand-new novels every month and be billed just $4.74 per book in the U.S. or $5.24 per book in Canada. That's a savings of at least 14% off the cover price! It's quite a bargain! Shipping and handling is just 50¢ per book in the U.S. and 75¢ per book in Canada.* I understand that accepting the 2 free books and gifts places me under no obligation to buy anything. I can always return a shipment and cancel at any time. Even if I never buy another book, the two free books and gifts are mine to keep forever.

235/335 HDN F45Y

Name	(PLEASE PRINT)	
Address		Apt. #
City	State/Prov.	Zip/Postal Code

Signature (if under 18, a parent or guardian must sign)

Mail to the **Harlequin® Reader Service:**
IN U.S.A.: P.O. Box 1867, Buffalo, NY 14240-1867
IN CANADA: P.O. Box 609, Fort Erie, Ontario L2A 5X3

**Want to try two free books from another line?
Call 1-800-873-8635 or visit www.ReaderService.com.**

* Terms and prices subject to change without notice. Prices do not include applicable taxes. Sales tax applicable in N.Y. Canadian residents will be charged applicable taxes. Offer not valid in Quebec. This offer is limited to one order per household. Not valid for current subscribers to Harlequin Special Edition books. All orders subject to credit approval. Credit or debit balances in a customer's account(s) may be offset by any other outstanding balance owed by or to the customer. Please allow 4 to 6 weeks for delivery. Offer available while quantities last.

Your Privacy—The Harlequin® Reader Service is committed to protecting your privacy. Our Privacy Policy is available online at www.ReaderService.com or upon request from the Harlequin Reader Service.

We make a portion of our mailing list available to reputable third parties that offer products we believe may interest you. If you prefer that we not exchange your name with third parties, or if you wish to clarify or modify your communication preferences, please visit us at www.ReaderService.com/consumerchoice or write to us at Harlequin Reader Service Preference Service, P.O. Box 9062, Buffalo, NY 14269. Include your complete name and address.

SPECIAL EXCERPT FROM

H HARLEQUIN®

SPECIAL EDITION

*Matteo Mendoza is used to playing second fiddle
to his brother Cisco…but not this time. Beautiful
Rachel Robinson intrigues both siblings, but Matteo
is determined to win her heart. Rachel can't resist the
handsome pilot, but she's afraid her family secrets might
haunt her chances at love. Can this Texan twosome find
their very own happily-ever-after on the range?*

Read on for a sneak preview of
MENDOZA'S SECRET FORTUNE by USA TODAY
bestselling author Marie Ferrarella, the third book in
THE FORTUNES OF TEXAS: COWBOY COUNTRY
continuity!

***

Matteo knew he should be leaving—and had most likely
already overstayed—but he found himself wanting to linger
just a few more seconds in her company.

"I just wanted to tell you one more time that I had a very
nice time tonight," he told Rachel.

She surprised him—and herself when she came right down
to it—by saying, "Show me."

Matteo looked at her, confusion in his eyes. Had he heard
wrong? And what did she mean by that, anyway?

"What?"

"Show me," Rachel repeated.

"How?" he asked, not exactly sure he understood what she
was getting at.

Her mouth curved, underscoring the amusement that was already evident in her eyes.

"Oh, I think you can figure it out, Mendoza," she told him. Then, since he appeared somewhat hesitant to put an actual meaning to her words, she sighed loudly, took hold of his button-down shirt and abruptly pulled him to her.

Matteo looked more than a little surprised at this display of proactive behavior on her part. She really was a firecracker, he thought.

The next moment, there was no room for looks of surprise or any other kind of expressions for that matter. It was hard to make out a person's features if their face was flush against another's, the way Rachel's was against his.

If the first kiss between them during the picnic was sweet, this kiss was nothing if not flaming hot. So much so that Matteo was almost certain that he was going to go up in smoke any second now.

The thing of it was he didn't care. As long as it happened while he was kissing Rachel, nothing else mattered.

***

Don't miss MENDOZA'S SECRET FORTUNE
by USA TODAY bestselling
author Marie Ferrarella,
the third book in
THE FORTUNES OF TEXAS: COWBOY COUNTRY
continuity!

Available March 2015, wherever
Harlequin® Special Edition books and ebooks are sold.

Copyright © 2015 by Marie Rydzynski-Ferrarella

HSEEXPO215

HARLEQUIN®
A *Romance* FOR EVERY MOOD™

**Stay up-to-date on all your
romance-reading news with the
Harlequin Shopping Guide,
featuring bestselling authors, exciting new
miniseries, books to watch and more!**

The newest issue will be delivered right to you
with our compliments! There are 4 each year.

Signing up is easy.

EMAIL

ShoppingGuide@Harlequin.ca

WRITE TO US

HARLEQUIN BOOKS
Attention: Customer Service Department
P.O. Box 9057, Buffalo, NY 14269-9057

OR PHONE

1-800-873-8635 in the United States
1-888-343-9777 in Canada

Please allow 4-6 weeks for delivery of the first issue by mail.

JUST CAN'T GET ENOUGH
ROMANCE
Looking for more?

Harlequin has everything from contemporary, passionate and heartwarming to suspenseful and inspirational stories.

Whatever your mood, we have a romance just for you!

Connect with us to find your next great read, special offers and more.

Facebook.com/HarlequinBooks
Twitter.com/HarlequinBooks
HarlequinBlog.com
Harlequin.com/Newsletters

HARLEQUIN
A *Romance* FOR EVERY MOOD™

www.Harlequin.com

SERIESHALOAD